THE NAMELESS WOMAN

The Nameless Woman
Copyright ©2025 by Ethan Cooley

All rights reserved. No part of this book may be reproduced or transmitted in any form or by any means whatsoever without written permission from the author.

This book is a work of fiction. Names, characters, places, and incidents are either the product of the author's imagination or are used fictitiously. Any resemblance to actual persons, living or dead, events, or locals is entirely coincidental.

ISBN: 979-8-9994157-4-5 (Hardcover)

ISBN: 979-8-9994157-3-8 (Paperback)

Contact Info: www.eecooley.com

Cover design: Ethan Cooley

Editors: Kim Autrey

First Edition

Also By E.E. Cooley

The Nameless Man

Prime Youth: Prisoners of the Masquerade
Prime Youth: Operation Turbulence

Bondage to Freedom

To all the beautiful souls we will never hear

PART 1: CONCEPTION

1

The line stretched as far as the eye could see. The abundance of life and hope in people a stark contrast to the barren landscape surrounding them. The ship was set to take this line of people off of Earth and into the stars, away from the unlivable planet.

Journalists and researchers had documented over the last thirty years the slow decline of the planet, and the solution proposed by the world powers. Some imposed birth bans, hoping to stop the population growth and save resources. Others turned to science, looking to strengthen plants that could survive the harsh environments. While others to medicine, hoping to create something that would allow the human body to still function in a low resource environment.

But none of the world's best scientists, doctors, or researchers found a solution. Collectively the world powers voted in favor of leaving the Earth; to live among the stars with the hope that after a few generations, the world would right itself, without the intervention of humans.

So the engineers set to work building spaceships capable of holding entire populations. For the first time in history all the world powers worked together, sharing knowledge and resources for the benefit of the human race.

Initially small teams were sent to space to construct what were called Worldships that everyone would live on. Smaller ships would then be used to bring the population to these

The Nameless Woman

Worldships. This proved too costly and timely a strategy, and with the acceleration of technology, the Worldships were able to be built on Earth with rockets that would allow the ships to leave the atmosphere and land back on Earth when it was deemed habitable again.

And this line of people was for one of the new Worldships, capable of holding 10,000 people each. The line stood in a transparent tunnel with a tall chain link fence surrounding both sides, armed guards stood just inside the fence wearing gas masks. Outside the fence stood beggars who were not chosen in the first round of selections to go on the Worldship, willing to trade anything for a spot in line. The guards along the fence constantly reminding everyone not to engage with anyone outside the fence. That was easier said then done when there were others outside the fence insisting everyone in line was making a mistake; that the government lied to everyone and the Earth was still habitable. Several of these people received warnings from the guards, who were allowed to use lethal force if necessary to protect the tunnel's occupants.

Other places along the fence had various groups of people praying, others quietly looking at the crowd, and lots crying. None of these people, however, stood near anyone that humanity had collectively called the Infected. A new virus, named the Alister Virus after the man who discovered it, had swept the world. Some survived, some were never infected, others died within days, and everyone else lived in wretched agony. Extreme body aches and muscle cramping, blood escaping the sinuses and mouth, food intolerances ranging from gluten, dairy, seafood, and even all three, headaches that would last for days, and constant hunger.

A cure had been discovered about two years after the first case of the Alister Virus was discovered, but the virus kept morphing, requiring more and more cures. So it was decided that everyone chosen in the first wave people to leave on the Worldships be isolated 4 months prior to their departure, ensuring they were free of any potential virus, not just the Alister Virus, but even the common cold. No virus or sickness was to come aboard any of the Worldships; the tunnel the biggest proponent of that plan.

One woman standing in line looked through the tunnel at one of the Infected pressed to the fence. Blood covered the front of his clothes and blood-filled gauze filled his nose as he slowly slid down the fence, groaning upon hitting the ground. The man looked utterly defeated, a flicker of hope was left as he reached out toward the tunnel, only to have his arm kicked by one of the guards. The man let out a scream, retracting his arm, only to lay against the fence and start crying.

The woman in line quickly looked away, guilt filling her not being able to help the man, but grateful for the tunnel's protection. She had gotten an early case of the Alister Virus before there was a cure, having to endure the symptoms for nearly three weeks. She did not want to have to go through that ever again.

The line started moving, and the woman picked up her small bag from the ground, moving with the line and setting it back down when the line stopped. Everyone in line had been given the exact same bag, instructed to put three days' worth of clothing inside to comply with weight limits for the ship. The bag had to completely close to be cleared.

The couple in front of the woman had been discussing which pair of heels the wife should keep. The husband had tried every conceivable way to fit both pairs between their two bags, but nothing worked. The discussion on which pair to keep had made the woman blush and turn away, wishing she was in a different part of the line.

Moving at an agonizing stop-and-go pace, the woman could feel the anticipation from the line building. Everyone was ready to leave, and so was she. After what felt like an eternity, she finally made it to the entrance gate. Her ID had been checked when she first entered the tunnel, but was checked once again before entering through the gate. The sliding door opened, and she entered with a group of ten others. They were instructed by flight attendants to empty their bags into trays for decontamination. The trays ran on a conveyor through the decontamination machine before everyone hastily refilled their bags, waiting with their group in another line. This line had multiple groups waiting to enter the ship.

The woman glanced up as she looked around the room, finding a transparent ceiling and the Worldship that dwarfed anything she had seen before. She quietly gasped, catching everyone's attention as they followed her gaze, being equally as stunned. Their astonishment was short lived as their attention was drawn back to the moving line.

As the woman's group reached the front of the line they were directed to one of two doors, each wide enough for one person to enter. Both doors led to the same small white room, just big enough to hold the group. A single large interior door and several holes in the wall were all that occupied the space. The outer doors closed with a hiss as a calming female voice came over a speaker saying, "Please close eyes and mouth for decontamination." Everyone complied, and three beeps replaced the woman's voice before white smoke was shot into the room. Some of the group nearly fell over from the force of the smoke, which lasted only a second.

Everyone's skin immediately felt sticky. Before anyone could touch their arms, the female voice said, "Please refrain from touching skin for ten minutes after decontamination, and welcome aboard Worldship Two." The interior door unlocked, sliding open with a hiss like the exterior doors. The group made their way inside the ship, grumbling about their itchy arms.

They were greeted inside by a long line of flight attendants, adorned in the Worldship signature light blue and yellow suits and hats. Everyone carried a bright smile on their faces as ten attendants left the line.

"Hey there," said a female flight attendant, a little over the top, walking up to the woman. "Welcome to Worldship Two. If you have your ID, I can find you your room?" The woman dug through her bag for her ID before handing it to the flight attendant, who pulled a handheld scanner from her belt, and upon scanning the ID, beckoned the woman to follow. "Isn't this so exciting!" said the flight attendant.

The woman thought she had way too much energy but cheerfully responded, "It is exciting."

"You're going to love your room, it's so cute." The flight attendant's heels clicked against the dull gray floor. The bland color continued through the rest of the ship, the only contrast coming from the white lights in the walls.

They walked along the hallway for a while as it ran the outer perimeter of the ship. Occasional port hole windows showed up on her left and a door every now and then on her right. Displays next to each door showed a map of the ship and where they were on it.

The two made light conversation which turned into the flight attendant babbling about all the interesting facts she had learned about the ship, which the woman tuned out when it seemed the flight attendant wasn't taking any breaths as she talked, only taking one when they stopped at a door the map indicated was toward the front of the ship. The doors slid open as they approached, revealing a hallway that wasn't much wider than the two of them side by side.

"A little tight, isn't it?" asked the woman.

"It is. This isn't your four hundred thousand square foot mansion back home." The flight attendant laughed. "The engineers had to utilize every square inch of this ship. It may be tight, but at least it's better than being back on Earth."

The woman agreed with the statement. She was so relieved when she was contacted about getting a spot on the first ships, celebrating by opening her dessert ration, which she had saved for just this kind of special occasion.

They made their way down the hallway, squeezing past

others as flight attendants showed them their rooms.

"Alright," said the flight attendant stopping at a door, just as excited as she was when the woman first met her. The woman could never act that chipper for so long, it'd probably make her mouth hurt too much from all the smiling.

The flight attendant took out her handheld scanner again, looking at the small screen for the door access code before entering it. "Here you go." She stepped back from the door and waved her arm, beckoning the woman inside.

The room was a small rectangle with no furniture or wall decorations. "Where is everything?" the woman asked.

"It's all in the walls. Let me show you." The flight attendant stepped around the woman. On the far wall, perpendicular to the door, she pulled a latch in the center of the wall, pulling down a couch with cushions. "Here you have your couch that also doubles as your take off seats. You have harnesses that pull out from underneath, and your monitor will also instruct you how to attach these on takeoff and landing." The flight attendant pointed to the screen on the opposite wall.

"What else does the screen do?" the woman stepped up to the screen.

"You can watch shows, do workouts, get the news, lot of things. You can even watch a real-time feed of our ship from cameras mounted all over the hull. The best part is it's voice activated. Just say 'monitor on' or whatever you call your monitor at home, and it will walk you through the rest. Now let's show you the bed."

On the adjacent wall with the door the flight attendant pulled down a latch in the middle of the wall to reveal a bed. "Here is your bed that can be down and not hit your couch, giving you space to sleep three if necessary. And flanking the bed is some storage space." The flight attendant opened the two narrow floor-to-ceiling doors.

"That's not much storage?" said the woman looking inside the cabinets not wide enough to fit more than five pieces of clothing.

"You're not getting more than what you brought on. And we don't have any stores on board, so you won't be buying anything new." Without skipping a beat, the flight attendant continued talking while she put up the bed. "But there's your room. Your access code that gets into your room is on your monitor. So make sure to memorize it before you leave. If you ever need anything, you can hit the call button next to the lights." She pointed to a circular button next to the rectangle button for the lights by the door. "Are there any other questions or needs I can take care of before I go?"

The woman looked around the room before replying, "I don't think so, thank you!"

"My pleasure." The flight attendant had the biggest smile on her face. "We do ask that everyone remain in their rooms until after takeoff. The screen will direct you when it's safe to do so. And on behalf of all the staff, we want to thank you for traveling on Worldship Two. Your contributions to society have not gone unnoticed, and we thank you for using them to ensure the survival of the human race with us, thank you." The flight attendant turned on her heal as the door slid open, walking out into the bustling hallway.

The woman was still shocked at the flight attendant's over-the-top cheeriness, at least compared to herself. Quickly throwing the thought out of her mind, she opened her bag and arranged the clothes in the cabinets, shoving the bag into the bottom of one before closing the door.

Sitting on the couch, the woman let out a breath she didn't realize she was holding. The room may have been a stark white box, but was a relief to know there wasn't a world of chaos outside the front door. That there wasn't a world of murderous people, who were walking viruses, all around her. She closed her eyes knowing she could freely walk around the ship, the safest she had been in years. No diseases, no viruses, and no sickness.

A light ding sounded in the room. The woman opened her eyes, finding the monitor was on. A countdown at the top read "Estimated Departure – 1:02:45" with pictures of the ship scrolling beneath it. These were clearly promotional photos, many of them used in the advertising of the Worldships, but some new ones too.

She had the urge to use the restroom, remembering the flight attendants asked no one to leave their rooms until takeoff. She got up to press the call button, but stopped halfway there, kicking herself that she treated herself like a kid in school. She didn't need to ask to use the restroom. The only problem, she didn't know where it was. She looked around for a map, about to go back to the hallway map she saw earlier when she had an idea.

"Monitor?" she asked.

The monitor dimmed and a red line filled the center of the screen. "Monitor here," said a calming female voice. The line moved like it would on an audio track, looking like a roller coaster. "Before I begin assisting you, would you like to set up your preferences?"

"No thank you, monitor."

"Alright, how can I assist you?"

"Where is the restroom, monitor?"

A map popped up on the monitor as blue dots started populating it. "The closest restroom to your location is here."

A red line was drawn from the woman's room to the restroom just down the hall. "Exit the room to your left, and it's the tenth door on your right. It will be marked on the wall."

"Thank you, monitor." The woman pressed the button to open the door.

"Everyone is instructed to stay in their cabins until after takeoff—"

"I can't wait." The woman exited the room, weaving in and out of traffic in the hallway. She found the restroom in the center of the hallway, discovering it to be a lot smaller then expected. There were only two stalls, one shower, and one sink, which seemed far too inadequate for everyone in the hallway it was most likely intended for.

The woman still had to use the restroom though, taking the one free stall. There was a hollow silence to the room, everything was made of stainless steel and echoes. As she closed the door, an almost deafening echo came from the flushing toilet in the next stall. "Ow" the woman mouthed touching her ears.

When she was done, she found a button on the wall to her left with a simple picture of toilet paper; no toilet paper was in sight anywhere. The button had a blue light lining the edge. Pressing it once, a strip of toilet paper exited a small slit next to the button. As she tore it off, the light around the button turned red. She pressed the button again and again, but nothing happened.

The woman remembered stories her grandmother would tell her, how she could buy as much toilet paper as she wanted. You could buy however much of whatever you wanted, no button prevented you from getting more. She held the long strand of toilet paper in front of her, frowning, hoping it would be enough. And by some miracle, she had just enough. She let out a breath before flushing the toilet, this time ready for the deafening echo.

After opening the stall door, the woman found another

woman leaning over the sink, one hand on the edge of the sink, the other on her stomach. "Are you alright?" the woman asked rushing over, discovering the bump on the other woman's stomach. "Oh, you're pregnant. Are you having contractions?"

The pregnant woman just nodded her head. After a moment, she took a deep breath and slowly exhaled. "I'm fine now." She slowly stood up, keeping one hand on her stomach.

"How far along are you?"

"I'm hopefully due in the next week or two. We'll see if space travel has any affect."

"I didn't think of that. Did they warn you about traveling while pregnant?"

"Not that I read or was told. But either way, I'm confident she'll be alright."

"It's a girl?"

"Yes." The pregnant woman looked at her stomach and rubbed it. "Her name is Amelia."

"That's a beautiful name."

"Thank you. Well I better get back. My husband will get worried if I'm not back soon." The pregnant woman did her coat up, concealing some of the bump underneath it.

"Of course, let me grab the door for you."

"Thank you."

As soon as the door opened, the hustle and bustle of the hallway burst inside. The pregnant woman waved bye as she exited, having to wait for an opening to get out. The woman closed the door, shutting her eyes and savoring the silence before washing her hands.

Bracing herself for the zoo outside, the woman opened the door, zigzagging through the maze of people. After passing at least two dozen giddy passengers and over-the-top flight attendants, she made it back to her room unscathed. Leaning against the door, she breathed another sigh of relief, hoping the crowds and noise were just because everyone was boarding.

"Monitor?"

A moment later the red line of the monitor appeared, and the screen jumped to life. "How may I assist you?"

"Could you put on some calming music, please?"

"Of course." A light piano started playing, and a grin spread across the woman's face as she closed her eyes, enjoying the music. After the song changed, she headed over to the couch, finding the monitor showed there were still fifty minutes before takeoff. Laying her head back, the woman quickly drifted off to sleep in the serene atmosphere of the bedroom.

The woman was abruptly awoken by a blaring alarm. Bolting up, she frantically looked around. The alarm stopped, and the monitor line appeared. "My apologies if I scared you, but you were not responding to the quieter alarms."

"What's going on?" The woman rubbed the sleep from her eyes.

"We are nearing takeoff. You need to put your takeoff harness on. Located under your seat." The monitor's line moved to the top of the screen as a diagram filled the rest of it, demonstrating how to attach the harness. As soon as she pulled the last strap tight, the same light ding sounded as the intercom came on, coming from speakers in the wall next to the lights as opposed to through the monitor's speakers.

"Good afternoon everybody, this is the captain speaking. My name is Captain Graham, and on behalf of all our staff, we'd like to welcome you aboard Worldship Two.

"By now you should all be strapped in for takeoff, but if you're still having trouble getting that harness attached, let your monitor know or hit the call button by your door, and one of our lovely flight attendants will be there to assist you momentarily.

"We do ask that everyone keep their harness on until after we've left the Earth's atmosphere. Your monitor will alert you when it's safe to unstrap, and I will come over the intercom to do the same.

"Additionally during takeoff, please keep both feet flat on the ground and your head resting against the back of your couch to avoid any injuries. We do have medical staff on board, but I would hate for you to start your trip off by seeing them.

"On behalf of all the world powers, we want to thank each and every one of you for your contributions to this society. By being selected to leave in the first wave of Worldships, you are among the best and brightest minds. You will be instrumental in the continuation of the human species, and it's an honor and privilege to be your captain in this momentous moment in history.

"Again, on behalf of all the staff, welcome aboard Worldship Two."

The woman sat back according to the captain's request as piano music slowly filled the room again. As the timer on the monitor got to one minute, a light ding accompanied each second. At five seconds, the ship shook as the engines fired up. The woman gripped the seat as all the engines came to full power, shaking the ship violently and drowning out the sound of the timer. The woman closed her eyes as the timer hit zero. She slowly sank further and further down into her seat, the pressure on her becoming heavier and heavier. The woman was worried she'd go right through the seat as she clutched it harder in the desperate attempt to know she was still alive. The feeling lasted an eternity, until finally the ship left the atmosphere. The pressure released, and the woman took several deep breaths, slowly releasing her teeth she hadn't realized she'd clenched, her jaw coming away sore.

A light ding sounded before the captain came over the intercom. "Attention all passengers, welcome to space. You may now remove your harnesses and walk about the ship at your leisure. We hope you enjoy your stay as we ensure the survival and continuation of the human race. Thank you."

The woman sat on the couch for several minutes to let her heart rate calm down. When it finally came back to a reasonable rate, she undid her harness, shoving it back into the storage slot under the seat.

She headed to the door wanting to explore the ship, bracing herself for the onslaught of people outside, and to her surprise found a very sparse hallway. Taking advantage of it, she headed toward the end of the hallway, exiting through the sliding door into the perimeter hallway that wrapped around the entire ship. The woman felt far less claustrophobic out here and enjoyed it while it lasted

Scanning the hallway, she found very few people walking about. The majority of them were pressed to the outside wall, gathered around porthole windows along the wall. She found two open windows in front of her, one at head height and the other near her knees, intended for children.

Outside was the beautiful landscape of space, stars twinkling in the distance. The woman's jaw dropped slightly at the sight of the Earth at the far edge of her view. Nothing in her life compared in beauty and vastness to what she was experiencing now. It was haunting while being spectacular. It made her feel so small. But then she looked closer at the Earth, finding far more patches of deserts than she remembered the Earth having. What was once green with forests and grass was now dead or dying. But the pictures were true to what satellites had taken pictures of in recent years.

The advertising for the Worldships always showed pictures of the Earth and how it was far from what many would recognize. At first it was shocking to everyone, some wouldn't even believe it. But after all the publicity over the years and the Earth slowly looking worse and worse as time went on, many accepted it as the new state of the Earth.

There were always skeptics of course, people who claimed the pictures were fake or governments were responsible. Every theory under the sun was refuted as baseless claims to prevent people leaving the planet. These skeptics were eventually collectively called Landers after a famous video of one of them. And looking at the Earth now, the woman wished the Landers could see what she was seeing, an Earth that was lost.

4

Using the maps at every intersection, the woman found her way to the food court. Her stomach grumbled as the double doors slid open, revealing a less than stellar attempt at a food court. Everything was the same stark white or dull gray as the rest of the ship. On both ends of the room sat restaurants that spanned the length of the room, similar to a food court. Some were very small while others were long. The only color in the room came from small signs above the start of the restaurant lines.

There were already several people waiting in a line to her left that temporary barriers forced her to join. She could see a long line of tables with flight attendants sitting in front of several boxes. When she reached the front of the line, a flight attendant directed the woman to an open spot at one of the tables.

"Good afternoon," said another chipper female flight attendant, "could I see your ID?"

"Of course. I'm glad I brought it." The woman handed the flight attendant her ID, who scanned it with her handheld scanner.

"Did you enjoy the flight?"

The woman shook her head. "Not really. I'm glad it's over."

"Flying in space for the first time can be rough." The flight attendant pulled a small circular screen from a box, pressing it to the scanner. After a moment, a green light on the scanner flashed accompanied by a chime. "Could you hold out your non-dominant hand please?" The flight attendant laid everything on the table and measured the women's left wrist. Grabbing a strap from a box behind her, she fed it through the bottom of the screen, creating a watch. The strap was elastic with magnets on either end to keep it attached. It hugged the woman's wrist firmly, but not so tight that it hurt. A message scrolled up the screen that read "Welcome to Worldship 2."

"Is that too tight?" asked the flight attendant.

"It's perfect." The woman examined the watch. "Thank you."

"Of course. The watch will let you buy food, check you into your room, and several other things. But there will be a video you can watch back in your room to explain everything."

"Awesome, thank you."

"Thank you," the flight attendant said with a huge smile. "Have a great day."

The woman walked around the tables, looking up and down at all the signs for something good. She spotted a green sign that said "Deli Sandwiches and Soup." After a bone-rattling ride to space, something easy on the stomach was all the woman wanted.

Walking over to the line, she was greeted by a far less over-the-top employee, a man with a black apron. "Good afternoon," he said walking up to the counter.

"Hi," said the woman, "what are my options here?" She pointed to trays of food inside clear rectangular cases across the counter, not seeing any signs to indicate the food available.

"We have ham and cheese." The man pointed to the first case on his left, going down the line. "Turkey and cheese, chicken and cheese, chili, and broccoli soup."

"Ooo, I'll do the broccoli soup, please."

"I just had that before I started my shift, it's wonderful. Just tap your watch to the scanner." The man motioned to a small metallic circle that sat on the right of the case, there was one on every case for all the different foods. The woman held her watch against the circle. A ding sounded, and a green light lit up behind the circle as the front of the case retracted down into the counter.

"That's fancy," said the woman grabbing a tray, only to find the soup wasn't a liquid but a solid, in the shape of a cube, that rattled inside the bowl.

"There's hot water to rehydrate the soup here." The man pointed to a metallic faucet next to the case, noticing the puzzled look on the woman's face.

"Rehydrate?"

"Yes. Most of our food is either freeze-dried or dehydrated. Just add some water, and your food is as fresh as ever."

"... it's soup though?"

"It tastes good, trust me," the man said with a smile.

The woman hesitantly moved her bowl under the hot water faucet, but nothing came out.

"There's another scanner on the front," said the man.

There was a small dot on the front face of the faucet. The same ding sounded, and a green light appeared in the small dot when she pressed her watch to it. And when she put her bowl underneath, the faucet dispensed a pre-determined amount of water.

Slowly the woman noticed the water being absorbed into the block of soup.

"Have a good day," said the man walking over to help a couple who had just walked up.

Still concerned about the legitimacy of dehydrated soup, the woman searched for a table, taking in her surroundings as she went. The ceiling was tall and arched, allowing for very few support pillars throughout the room. Large monitors sat across these arches that everyone could see from wherever they were sitting.

The woman grabbed a seat near the center of the room, away from the lines at both ends of the room, which were slowly drawing more people.

Picking up the spoon that sat on her tray, she poked at the block of soup, which was now soft, almost spongy. But the water was still being absorbed. This was not the type of meal she'd imagined, that was until the steam from the water started smelling like the soup she'd gotten.

While she waited for it to rehydrate, she watched the scrolling images on the monitors. In the right corner was the time, 5:46pm. Promotional images of the Wordship played behind the time. A smiling family in their room no different to hers, just bigger. Laughing groups of people eating food in the same room she was. Flight attendants and their pilots all smiling for a group photo.

The wails of a crying child pulled her attention away from the monitor. A boy, no more than five years old, stood in one of the lines as his parents tried to beckon him forward. The family started walking toward a table, hoping to encourage their son to follow, when he threw his tray on the floor. The father immediately scrambled over to pick up the food while the mom stood with their daughter, embarrassment all over her face.

The woman turned away from the situation, not wanting to embarrass the family anymore with another set of staring eyes. She instead found her soup nearly ready to eat.

Poking at the spongy block of soup, her spoon easily tore in as it nearly disintegrated. A moment later the soup was back to its liquid-based form she was familiar with.

It smelled far better than she was expecting; and after hesitantly taking a bite, tasted much better than she was expecting too. She ate her soup in silence, the closest person sitting five seats down from her. The room was oddly silent for how many people were in it by the time the woman finished her soup. About 2000 occupied the 5000-seat room, but the majority of them were all hushed as they spoke, except the over-the-top flight attendants, which could be heard all across the room.

Just as she was about to stand up, the woman felt her watch vibrate. At the same time, the monitors on the wall gave off three soft dings. Both popped up with the same message:

"Passengers. Welcome Meeting in the Garden in 15:01:57. Attendance: All Passengers"

Taking the time left on the countdown, the woman calculated the meeting to start at nine the next morning. She scooped up her tray and went to find a place to put it, intent on finding where the garden was.

Along the side walls at the center of the room were places to put your trays. Big signs above them read: NO TRASH. ALL FOOD MUST BE EATEN OR SHARED. Lower down on the sign it read: SHARE TABLE, with an arrow pointing to the table below. There were already plates of half finished and unfinished food scattered about the multiple share tables. It surprised the woman that so much food hadn't been eaten, and this was the first day on the ship. She was too full to eat anymore and wondered if any of the food would go to waste as she put her tray up.

Next to the tray tables was a door, the monitor to the side of it read: Garden. Underneath in a bordered box it read: Ready. A surprised smile crossed the woman's face as she headed over to the door. Its double doors slid open, and she walked into a vestibule as the doors closed behind her. Another set of doors in front of her waited to open until the first doors had fully closed, revealing a vast sea of trees.

A path wound around the trunks branching at multiple points; the trees brushed the domed ceiling high above. The woman followed the path, wide enough for four people, until it came to a clearing just as big as the cafeteria. A stage sat in the center while planters of colorful flowers lined the edge of the clearing. The woman stopped, the scene was so peaceful as she took it in. The color and life so abundant, especially as she noticed the domed ceiling above the clearing was glass. The stars beyond twinkled their beautiful light. It was an oasis in the midst of chaos, at least the woman thought it was chaos. So much to do and manage, she couldn't imagine having to handle the logistics of the ship. Getting enough food and water, sorting out rooms, having enough fuel for the trip. It made her head hurt just thinking about it.

She took a deep breath and looked back at the stars to calm down. Taking off across the clearing to the opposite side; following one of the multiple paths she thought would take her out of the garden.

Coming to the opposite end of the room from where she entered, she found another set of double doors that opened to a long hallway. Checking the map on the outside of the door to verify, she took a right, following the hallway along the perimeter of the garden, heading back to the door she entered the cafeteria through. The line to get in, however, was stretched out the door, many faces showing their hunger and displeasure at having to wait, some of the children in line even worse.

The woman made her way back to her room, using her watch to open the door instead of her access code. A wave of exhaustion hit her as she closed the door. The monitor only read 6:25, but her body's clock acted like it was midnight. She pulled out her one pair of pajamas and threw them on groggily before pulling her bed down from the wall. The sheets were cold at first, but by the time they warmed up, the woman was fast asleep, forgetting to turn the light off. The monitor, using its camera, was able to detect the woman was asleep and turned the lights off.

The woman could hear the roar from the garden long before she entered. A line stretched out the door, and she was in the middle of it. She played with her hands as the line crawled forward. When she made it to the garden doors, the sound was muffled thanks to the trees, but when she made it through to the clearing, the sound was deafening. Chairs had been arranged facing the stage, filled with all ages from babies on up. It was a mad house of flight attendants directing passengers to seats, babies crying, and families waving and yelling for each other.

A flight attendant waved the woman down to the edge of the clearing, near the path to the cafeteria. She got one of the last seats in the room before everyone else was filed into the overflow seating on the cafeteria.

With everyone sitting down, the chaos calmed just a little; it was difficult to have a conversation with the person next to you. The woman didn't know anyone sitting around her and chose to keep to herself. The people directly next to her were talking with their families and weren't a bother to her at all. As she looked around at several other families in the seats around her, the woman longed to have family to talk to.

She focused her attention on the stage before her thoughts could drift any more. She found an octagon of monitors standing tall above the stage, all of them with a countdown. On the stage was a large cloth-covered structure with a podium in front, facing the woman. Four poles with cameras sat on the corners of the stage facing the hidden structure.

A minute before the countdown hit zero, two men stepped out from a forest path to the side of the stage. One in a suit and another in nurse scrubs. As the timer hit zero the man in the suit walked up the steps and stood behind the podium.

"Good morning, everyone," the man said, and the crowd began to die down. "My name is Peter Graham. I have the privilege and honor of being the captain of Worldship Two. As the captain it is my responsibility, along with my crew, to ensure your safety while you are aboard this ship. You've already met some of our lovely flight attendants as you boarded. Should you need any help, don't hesitate to ask them, or any of the rest of my crew wearing blue and yellow suits with the Worldship Two pin on their left breast."

The captain looked down at his notes, taking a moment to pause before continuing. "I have a few items I wanted to make everyone aware of at this meeting, the first being our plan." The captain pulled a clicker from the podium and looked up to the monitors above him, finding his face replaced with a graphic of the Earth. "Right now, ten Worldships, one of them being us, are situated just outside the Earth's atmosphere." Ten little Worldships popped up around the Earth. "Forty more ships across the Earth are in various stages of completion. We will stay in the Earth's atmosphere until all the World Ships are completed and launched. Then we will all leave together."

A few murmurs came from the crowd as many people were not told this, though many did not ask and simply signed the paperwork in desperation to be chosen to get a spot on a Worldship.

"It will be nine months until all the ships are completed and launched. After that we will all take off together. And I'm sure one of the first questions you'll have is about food. Don't worry, we'll be resupplied with food before our journey. And we'll also have ships carrying extra food that will fly along side

The Nameless Woman

us, you have no need to worry about running out of food."

More murmurs rose around the room as concerns and questions floated through the air. The captain waited for the noise to quiet down before continuing. "Now that we're all up to speed on the logistics of our travel, let's talk about your stay here on Worldship Two. If you haven't already, everyone should have received a watch. This watch will allow you access into your room, to get food, update you with messages from the crew and I, and much more. You can watch a video about all your watch is capable of just by asking your monitor.

"If you haven't gotten a watch yet, some of our lovely flight attendants will be by the stage to hand them out. Remember, you can't get any food without it, so make sure to pick one up.

"In addition to the cafeteria, there is a bar located on the opposite end of the ship from us." A map of the ship filled the monitors with a dotted line that started at the garden, leading to a room on the very front of the ship. "The bar, along with several other rooms, will be open twenty-four seven. Check the monitors in front of any room to verify hours of operation. And on that note, there is no curfew on the ship." Several kids in the audience reacted with cheers and excitement. "All we do ask is that if you are traveling through a residential corridor at night, that you keep your voice down. The rooms are unlikely to have outside noise make their way inside, but just out of curtesy, we ask you keep your voice down.

"And now for our final topic. This is the most important topic we'll discuss today because it affects your well-being and potentially your life. As stated in your contract, on Worldship Two child birth is forbidden." The captain paused to let that point sink in, an eerie silence covered the room. "When we built the world's Worldships, we designed them to store enough food only for the passenger count at the time of boarding. Any additional passengers were not accounted for in food calculations. These passengers would take food not intended for them, stealing it from others who need it.

"Now the one question some of you may be asking is how will the human race continue if we don't repopulate? This is where the DNA test you took to apply comes in. Scientists have been looking over every single person's DNA for the most ideal traits to continue the next generation with. Our scientists are still looking over the data and will decide once we've had some time to acclimate to the ship, but be assured that within the next month, we will have people chosen to create the next generation."

The captain paused again, taking a drink from a cup hidden in the podium. Only a few murmurs floated through the crowd, but the majority were dead silent as the captain continued. "Now unfortunately... we have a problem. Some of you did not read the contract you signed. It explicitly stated that no one was to be pregnant, at any stage, if they were to be chosen for a Worldship. Some of you chose not to listen and are now in violation of your contract."

The man in nurse scrubs made his way up the stairs, pulling the tarp off the structure on the stage. Underneath was a domed cage. And inside the cage was a woman, naked, strapped to a medical bed, gagged, and situated like she was about to give birth. In fact, she was pregnant. The cameras on the stage extended up so they could see over the woman's stomach. They zoomed in as the woman frantically looked around her, struggling against her restraints. Several gasps came from the audience, and parents covered their children's eyes.

"What is this?" a man yelled.

"There are children here!" cried a woman.

"Then this will be a good lesson on consequences for your children, ma'am," said the captain calmly. The crowd started to grow louder, but the speakers increased their volume as the captain continued. "There are consequences for those who don't follow the rules. This is the same across all the

Worldships."

"That was never in the contract!" yelled a man standing up.

"It was if you read it," said a snarky woman.

"I did read it and that wasn't in there. He's lying." The man jabbed a finger at the captain.

"He's not lying," said the snarky woman as she stood up.

And then everyone started standing up. The voices all melding together, impossible to tell how many agreed with the man or the snarky woman.

The woman didn't know where to focus on and found her attention drawn to the monitors. The pregnant woman, she realized, was the same one she had met in the bathroom just yesterday.

The nurse sat down on a rolling chair in front of the pregnant woman, preparing various devices and tools, acting oblivious to the uproar around him. The woman examined what tools the nurse was preparing, and when she put it together, gunshots rang out all over the room.

Buzzing sounded over the crowd as everyone darted to the ground. The noise was even louder as more voices joined in, this time with screams of terror. The woman sat on her knees in front of her chair, and looking over the seat backs saw armed guards lining the edge of the clearing as they exited the tree line.

"Quiet!" The captain's voice boomed over the chaos. Everyone put their hands over their ears, and the room promptly calmed down. Only a few people crying, mainly children, sprinkled the crowd.

Most people turned to see the captain, who was adjusting his suit and tie.

"My apologies," said the captain. "But I was worried that would turn into a very big fight. And I didn't want anyone to get hurt. I hope you'll forgive me." The room was now completely silent. Only the very faint sound of the pregnant woman struggling against her restraints.

"Now, as I was saying. There are consequences for those that came onto this ship knowingly being pregnant, as this woman is." The captain waved his hand toward the pregnant woman. "She cannot have this baby because it will steal the resources and food of another passenger, potentially more. And I cannot see any of my passengers die because of that. There are consequences for those on a Worldship that do not follow the rules. Our survival is at stake, people. The continuation of the human race rests in our hands, and we cannot let anyone down."

There was a thick tension that covered the room. The woman looked around, finding several people on the edge of their seats in various states of arrest. The captain waited a very long minute before continuing.

"You may begin the procedure."

The nurse nodded to the captain, and in that same instant, six people from around the room jumped up and ran toward the stage. Every one of them, as soon as they were out of their row and in an aisle, were immediately shot by the guards. They were shot with rubber bullets, but everyone still cried out as they tumbled and slid across the ground. The crowd covered their ears as guards rushed down the isles to handcuff all the runners. In the chaos, a man from the front row darted toward the stage, jumping up the stairs three at a time when the captain caught him at the top step. There was a struggle that ended with the captain pinning the man on the ground before guards were able to take the man away.

The captain stood up, adjusting his suit and combing his hair back in place. After the guards had escorted their runners out of the room, the captain motioned for the nurse to begin again.

The nurse fired up a machine before walking over and removing the pregnant woman's gag. Her screams of terror, struggle, and cries for help were the only noise that filled the room. The woman's stomach churned as she knew what was about to happen.

"You can't do this," a woman yelled.

"You'll regret this," cried a man.

The next couple of minutes were a complete blur as the nurse used the devices to extract the baby from the womb. The woman's bloodcurdling cries lasted so long they were ingrained in everyone's brain, never to be forgotten. As the procedure ended, the nurse casually put his tools away and turned the machines off. The now not-pregnant woman began to cry, completely defeated as she stopped struggling against the restraints.

People began vomiting all throughout the crowd, in turn causing more people to vomit.

The woman clutched her stomach as she began thinking about what that woman was going to name her child when the captain stepped back up to the podium and the monitors turned off.

"I know for some of you that was hard to watch. But that was necessary to ensure none of us have to starve...or worse. I will protect the lives of my passengers." The captain became more enthusiastic as he continued. "No matter what we go through, no matter what storms we weather, I will ensure your well-being above all else!"

Scattered applause erupted—and within seconds the entire room exploded with roaring cheers and clapping that lasted well over five minutes. People even stood up. As the woman sat there, unsure how to respond, she noticed several people throughout the crowd not clapping, their body language showing they hadn't simply stopped clapping.

When the crowd finally died down, the captain continued. "For those of you that are pregnant and would like to ensure your neighbor is able to get their food, we have doctors waiting to take you to our medical ward." The captain waved down the stairs to a group of nurses who all cheerfully waved at the crowd. "I understand that this is a big decision to make, so I completely understand if you need some time before your procedure. But if anyone is ready, you may stand up and follow these nurses out."

Several women immediately stood up, others slowly stood, while some hesitated. A few husbands begged their wives not to go, some even crying as they walked toward the nurses. There were a couple husbands who were grabbed by the crowd if they prevented their wives from going up. When all the women had gotten up that wanted to, another round of applause broke out that lasted until the nurses escorted the sizable group out of the clearing.

"Make sure that we congratulate every single one of them the next time you see them. You've just been in the presence of heroes.

"Now the last thing before you go. My staff will be putting birth control in all of the bathrooms, as well as delivering some to every single room throughout the day today. You will all also be counted as heroes for making this sacrifice of not having any children. But that is all for today. You may return to the ship. Enjoy the rest of your day."

Everyone stood up as the captain walked off the stage. The woman sat still trying to process everything she had just witnessed. She wanted desperately to get up and leave, but she would turn into a wreck if she tried leaving in the sea of people.

With the crowd clearing, she could see through to the stage as a single soul cautiously walked up the stairs. The man took his coat off and laid it over the woman as he unstrapped her from the bed. And after messing with the machine on the stage, pulled out the container that held the contents of the woman's womb. He gently handed it to her as she clutched it to her chest. Her crying moans carried over the last of the crowd as they dispersed from the room and guards approached the stage. The man on the stage started crying as he slowly made his way down the stairs.

The Nameless Woman

The woman stared at these events with heartbreak bursting from every fiber of her being. As tears started running down her face, she quickly swiped them away, darting out of her chair. Her cheeks flushed as people stared at her, and the tears didn't stop. There were few people left from the crowd, allowing the woman to zigzag around everyone. She walked as fast as she could without running, heading straight to her room. The entire time one name repeated itself over and over in the woman's mind; the name that woman had picked for her child, Amelia.

The woman hadn't come out of her room in a week, of her own will that is. Her first visitor was a Worldship staff member to drop off the birth control. She got out of bed, collected the box from the staff member, put it on one of the storage cabinets, and got back in bed, sluggish with every step. This was the next day after the ship-wide meeting in the garden. The images she saw, frozen in her mind.

The monitor turned on at the end of the day when the woman still laid in bed. An alert was also given to the staff when the woman's watch hadn't been scanned to get any food.

On the third day, three staff, one a doctor, used their emergency medical clearance code to enter the room. The woman was in no state to rebuke this invasion of privacy she thought it was, instead, only pulling the covers up over her more.

The three staffers all hesitated as to who should speak first, but more importantly what to say. The doctor finally asked, "Excuse me, but we've been notified that you haven't had a meal in the last three days. We'd like to run a few tests to ensure your well-being."

"Are you going to strip me naked and do this in front of the entire ship?" asked the woman with no emotion or soul in her words.

All the staff laughed. "We won't do that to you," said the doctor. "Unless you get pregnant and plan to have a baby on board." The staff laughed again.

One of the staff, a woman, spoke up. "Those public displays are only for those murderous liars."

The woman thought about why the other pregnant women who went with the nurses after the speech weren't considered murderous liars, but she had so little energy that thought went no further, especially as the doctor asked several questions and examined her. When he was done the doctor concluded she needed lots of water and some food, both of which were ordered and brought to her room.

"I encourage you to eat regularly," said the doctor. "I know what you may have seen wasn't the most pleasant to watch, but we can't have you depriving yourself of food because of it."

"Are you done?" asked the woman as kindly as her tired mind allowed.

"Unless anyone else has anything?" the doctor asked looking toward the other staff who both shook their heads.

"Could you please leave then?"

"Of course," said the doctor hesitantly, "have a good day."

As the door closed the name Amelia popped back into the woman's head, and she started crying. Not because of what had happened, but because that woman had already chosen a name for her child, a child she wanted to have, and would never have the opportunity to know her own name.

The woman pulled the blankets over her head and bawled until she fell asleep in a puddle of her tears.

A week later the woman crawled out from under her sheets, dragging herself down the hall to use the restroom. She made sure to do this at night, at least what the ship considered night when all the lights dimmed. Because in space, there wasn't much of a day or night. She didn't want to interact with anyone, especially in her state of disarray.

This bathroom trip was different though. The woman was worried, more than worried, in a panic. She was long past due having her period. The two thoughts running around her mind were she was pregnant, or space was messing with her cycle.

She quietly opened the bathroom door, thankful to find herself alone. She grabbed a pregnancy test next to the sink and waited the agonizing eternity for the test results. She sat on top of the toilet seat, her legs pulled up to her chest, hugging them. When the result finally came, the test fell out of her hands. She was pregnant.

The woman was ecstatic, overjoyed, but absolutely terrified and mortified. She wanted to have this baby. She needed to have this baby. Not for any righteous reason, she just needed to have it for her own sake.

She saw herself up on the stage, naked in front of the entire ship, having the contents of her womb removed for everyone to see. The screams she heard pierced her ears, and she covered them, trying to block out the inaudible sound.

All the woman wanted to do was curl up into a ball on the

floor, hide away from everyone until her baby would be born. But she could only cry, her sobs echoing off the walls. She desperately wanted to curl up on the floor, but it didn't seem the most sanitary to do it on the bathroom floor. She would have laughed at herself for thinking of cleanliness at a time like this. But all she could do was cry. Every possibility of her child's life ran through her head. From growing up safe and secure aboard the ship, to hiding in secret, to getting off the ship and allowing her child to grow up on the Earth, even if it was a barren landscape of horrid infected people. Her grip around her legs tightened the more she cried, clawing her fingernails and nearly breaking through her pants. When she could cry no more, she had only one thought, no one was going to stop her from having her baby.

PART 2: FIRST TRIMESTER

Twenty-six days after the all-passenger meeting in the garden, the pregnant women who had their babies aborted, as well as others who made the decision after the meeting, were paraded around the ship and celebrated for their act. Passengers lined the outer hallway of the ship as the women were escorted by everyone, waving, smiling, and laughing.

After too many people came to her room asking if she was alright and bringing her food, the woman decided to crawl out of her bed and attend the parade, only to appease the staff members that kept barging into her room at all hours of the day.

Watching from the back of the crowd, the woman's stomach churned. Not from being in the crowd, but because it didn't seem right. How many women had wanted to have their children, and instead, were forced to abort it like the pregnant woman she had met.

As the parade approached the woman, the group of women had grown sizably from those that initially went at the meeting, easily double. Most of them waved and smiled like this was homecoming or a beauty pageant. But the woman was able to pick out several among the crowd with somber faces. These women still waved but were relegated to the center of the parade crowd. Unless you were looking closely, you would never be able to pick out these depressed-looking women.

Why these women looked that way wasn't clear as there were many possible reasons. The women regretted what they did; they had recently had the procedure and were still in pain; they didn't like all this attention; or they simply were mopey looking people? Either way the woman noticed all of them were in the center of the crowd, away from most eyes.

As the parade continued, the cheering got even louder, and that's when the woman saw the captain. He walked at the rear of the parade, waving and smiling like the rest of it. The crowd went absolutely crazy as he walked by. People screamed they loved him, others whistled or hollered, all the sound echoing off the walls. It became too much for the woman that she covered her ears. The crowd didn't die down until the captain was well past the bend in the hallway, and then the crowd dispersed.

The woman quickly turned around, making her way back to her room as quickly as her legs could carry her. Closing the door to her room, she leaned back against it, closing her eyes as she viewed the parade again in her mind.

Going through the memories in her mind, she realized she didn't remember seeing the pregnant woman from the stage in the parade. It had been almost a month since she had her forced abortion, she should have been more than alright. But what if something had happened, what if there was a complication, what if she died?

The thoughts overwhelmed her, and she became queasy, heading to the restroom. The hallway was a swarm of people returning from the parade, but this was no time to be slowed down. As politely as she could, she pushed her way through the crowd, storming into the bathroom, and finding the first available stall to puke her guts out. She had started eating again and was thankful she wasn't dry heaving, but it was still unpleasant.

"Oh dear," said another woman rushing to pull the woman's hair up. "I'm sorry, you got some on your hair." When the woman could finally talk again, she started quietly sobbing. "It'll be alright dear." The other woman rubbed the woman's back. "Here, let's get you cleaned up."

They made their way to the sink and began washing the woman's hair. "Thank you," said the woman looking through the mirror at the brown-haired woman helping her.

"Of course. I happen to be pretty experienced with this?"

"You get sick a lot?"

"No." The brown-haired woman chuckled. "I have three daughters."

"They get sick a lot?"

"It just comes with having children. First they puke on you, then you're holding their hair as they puke."

The woman started thinking about what it would be like to raise a child before crying, hiding her face in the sink.

"You'll be alright dear," said the brown-haired woman rubbing the woman's back.

The woman wanted to say she wouldn't. Spill her secret for some sympathy, for some help. She had kept her secret inside for too long. But all that came out was, "why are you being so kind to me?"

"Because I can see that you're in need, dear. Here you go, all clean. Now let's dry you off." The women went over to the air blower and dried off. "There we go, all better now."

"Yes," said the woman running her hand through her hair. "Thank you."

"Of course, happy to help." The brown-haired woman smiled. "Hey, I'm having a little get together tonight in my room, 649 at six o'clock. Are you doing anything tonight?"

"I appreciate the offer," the woman replied quickly, "but I do have plans tonight." They awkwardly stared at each other a moment before the woman headed for the door. "I appreciate your help," she said, grabbing the door handle.

"Burdens are hard to carry alone," said the brown-haired woman. The woman didn't move her hand off the door handle.

"And why do you say that?" the woman asked trying to hide as much of the nervousness in her voice.

"I would hate to see you do this alone."

The woman didn't know how to respond and left the bathroom, almost in a daze walking back to her room. Was that an undercover staffer that found out she was pregnant? And if it was, how had they found out? She flushed the pregnancy test down the toilet; it should have been destroyed. Or was she already showing and not been careful enough with hiding it?

The questions kept pouring through her mind, an unending bombardment. Until one question made her stop, why did she invite her over tonight? Being nice could just be acting. But if she really was out to stop her from having her child, why wouldn't she have just stopped her there? Was she feeling out the situation? Did she not want to cause a scene with everyone still milling around from the parade?

Her head hurt as the woman laid in her bed, unsure what thoughts were correct, insane, or outrageous. There was a thought inside of her to go to the brown-haired woman's place though. Something she couldn't explain. But she ignored it, wrestling with the implications of her conversation, driving herself crazy before succumbing to sleep.

The woman thanked the attendant at the soup line and walked with her tray to find a table. On her way to her usual spot, she eyed the brown-haired woman, sitting across from the woman's spot. That was the fifth time that had happened this week alone. Last week was seven. After changing what times she went to get food, she still managed to run into her every day.

Spinning on her heels, confused, annoyed, and worried, she found a seat as far away from the brown-haired woman as possible.

She ate her soup as quickly as she could without attracting attention to herself, getting up and putting her tray on the opposite side of the room from where the brown-haired woman was facing.

Leaving the room she half expected the flight attendants to gang up on her. Or for the security team to grab her on her way back to her room. But neither of those happened. When she got back to her room, she nearly collapsed in bed from exhaustion. This constant fear was breaking her down.

Every day she stayed in the food court less and less, eating her food faster and faster. Always looking over her shoulder to see if anyone was following her. Hiding out in the bathroom just to get away from her room.

The woman rolled over onto her back, staring at the ceiling. Looking around at her room she wasn't just exhausted; she was going insane. Seeing the same four walls all day,

The Nameless Woman

playing the same games and watching the same shows on the monitor, the woman needed something different. Then the thought of the brown-haired woman came to mind, specifically her invitation.

This time when thinking about her though, there wasn't as much fear as usual. Not of the woman herself but of her invitation. And then the thought struck her, she was stuck in space. There was no way to get back to the Earth short of overtaking the Worldship, finding a pilot, and surviving any resistance to the takeover. Her child would never be born. No matter how many scenarios she ran through, every one ended with either her dead or not being able to carry her child to birth.

And surprisingly, those thoughts didn't scare her as much as she thought they should have. There was an unreal amount of peace about her situation. Not that she wasn't scared, angry, frustrated, and worried, but normally it completely confiscated her life when she thought these things.

She laid her hands on her stomach, rubbing it, thinking about this child she could have. She whispered, "If there is a way for you to be born, I will do everything to ensure that happens... But it may very well be that I don't get to hold you. That I don't get to raise you. I don't get to kiss your face." Tears started running down the woman's face. "I didn't realize this ship wouldn't let me have you, and I'm sorry for that. I'm sure you would have been beautiful." The woman was overwhelmed by tears as she clutched her stomach.

And when there were no more tears to cry, she sat up, wiping her face off. The time on the monitor read 6:12pm. Maybe the brown-haired woman was having another party tonight. And if she was out to ensure she didn't bring her child to term, then maybe it would be better to get it over with than prolong the inevitable.

Still remembering the room from the invitation, the woman headed to the bathroom to clean herself up and headed toward the party

10

The woman pressed the doorbell on the monitor outside the door. A moment later, the door slid to the side, revealing the brown-haired woman.

"Hi," she said surprised. "I'm so glad you're here."

"I hope I'm not intruding," said the woman, "but I wanted to take you up on that party offer you gave me?"

"Yes, yes," said the brown-haired woman waving her in. "Come in, come in. We're actually having a party tonight."

"Looks like I came on the right night."

"Yes, you did."

The room was very similar to the woman's room. A monitor was on the left wall as you entered. A couch across from the monitor, and a bed on the wall to the right of the door. The room was wider though, allowing for a door to the right of the couch.

"So these are a few of my friends," said the brown-haired woman waving toward a man and a black-haired woman.

"You shouldn't introduce us," said the man with a gruff voice.

"I think it's alright if she knows our names. What's the—"

"No names," said the man adamantly. And the brown-haired woman obliged without any concern or rebuttal, which seemed odd to the woman.

"Oh, I almost forgot. We have a rule when we party. We don't party with the clock. We party till we're done. So, no watches in here."

"Oh, ok." The woman began taking her watch off and noticed that the monitor wasn't on at all, not even its sleep mode that had a faint clock in the background.

The brown-haired woman took the watch and stuck it in a bag in a closet, turning around and continuing the conversation like nothing had happened. "So, this is my family. We were all chosen in the first wave to be on a Worldship, so they gave us a room together." A look toward the man told the brown-haired woman not to say any more. "Alright, so—"

The monitor came on with the words "IMPORTANT BROADCAST" fading in and out of the screen. "Attention all passengers," said a woman through the monitor, "please make your way to the nearest monitor for an important broadcast. Thank you."

"What do you think that's about?" asked the black-haired woman.

"I don't know," said the brown-haired woman before looking back at the woman. "Here, take your shoes off, make yourself comfortable while we wait for the broadcast." The couch had already been pulled out, so the man and the brown-haired woman pulled out the bed. The man and the black-haired woman sat on the couch while the brown-haired woman sat with the woman on the edge of the bed.

A countdown began on the monitor, starting at sixty seconds. The room was dead silent, nobody moved as the countdown made its way to zero, the view changing to the captain on the bridge of the ship.

"Good evening, everyone," said the captain, throwing his arms open. "Thank you for making time for this important announcement, because we have some exciting news. After much research, our scientists have given us the list for who will continue on the next generation." Applause came from just outside where the camera could see, and the captain continued when they were finished. "As you could hear I have some people with me. So, let's introduce our lucky winners."

The captain introduced couples the woman didn't know. Some of them were married. Others were unrelated, just two random people were chosen to have a baby together. That seemed odd to the woman. Not that she was a stickler for only married couples having babies, but it's just something she wouldn't do. But when she started thinking about it from the viewpoint of the scientists, it made a little more sense. If it was purely based on genetics, then you'd want the two best candidates to have a baby together.

"And finally," said the captain after the slew of at least two dozen couples, "my wife and I." More applause filled the room as the captain's wife walked into view, both putting their arms around each other. "And that, everyone, are the lucky candidates to continue on the next generation." Another round of applause, this one the loudest and longest of them all, filled the room.

"Tomorrow morning," continued the captain, "we will have a parade followed by a celebratory brunch. We'll have special food and desserts for this occasion so make sure you don't miss it. Thank you everyone for tuning in tonight to this historic moment on Worldship Two. Now, I think we all have some work to do." The captain looked across the room, receiving nervous laughs as everyone filed out of the room, and the feed died.

The room was silent a moment before the man remarked, "those are all the rich and elites that were chosen."

"How do you know?" asked the woman, surprising herself with how quickly and confidently she asked.

"Do you watch the news? Every one of those people boasted when they were chosen for a Worldship. The news channels wouldn't stop covering them. They were all given the nice rooms on the ship. With a private bathroom and shower. Lots more room." The man shook his head.

"How did you find this out?" asked the woman.

"We've done some digging," said the brown-haired woman. "The richer or more famous you were the better accommodations you got."

"They're trying to control the population," said the black-haired woman.

All of this was making the woman's mind go crazy, making her hold her head.

"It's alright dear," said the brown-haired woman, putting a reassuring hand on her back. "It will all start to make sense soon."

"Is that before or after you tell her about his dream?" asked the black-haired woman.

The woman pulled her face out of her hands. "What dream?" she asked, looking around at everyone.

"The sooner we tell her the better," said the man.

"Not always," said the brown-haired woman.

"I think in this situation, sooner is better than later," said the black-haired woman.

"What dream?" the woman asked again.

The room was silent a moment before the brown-haired woman said, "Ok... You can tell her."

"You're pregnant," said the man without hesitation.

"I'm-I'm," stammered the woman.

"We're not going to turn you in," said the brown-haired woman quickly.

"Probably should have led with that," added the black-haired woman.

"I've never seen any of you before," said the woman. "You don't know anything about me."

"I had a dream," started the man. "A few weeks back. There was a woman, who I now know is you, and you were pregnant."

"That's not possible," the woman said at just above a whisper.

"I also had an urge," said the brown-haired woman. "After

hearing about the dream to go wait in the restroom for you."

"You couldn't know which one I would go to." The woman slowly stood up from the bed. "We're on opposite sides of the ship."

"After our interaction in the bathroom, I told him your description, and he said it matched you perfectly from his dream."

"No, no. You just saw me through the monitors." The woman backed up against the wall, slowly sliding toward the door.

The brown-haired woman got up, blocking the door. "I know this is a lot to take in. But we want to help—"

"Help?" The woman backed away from the brown-haired woman, edging toward the corner of the room. "You just want to take my baby."

Everyone in the room roared a protest against the woman's claim.

"We do not want to kill your baby," bellowed the man.

"You just want to turn me in because I'm a murderer." Tears ran down the woman's face as she backed into the corner of the room.

"You are not a murderer," said the black-haired woman.

"Then why are you surrounding me!" the woman screamed as she slid down the wall, hugging her knees to her chest as she collapsed to the floor. "You're not taking my baby!" she screamed before breaking into an uncontrollable crying fit.

Everyone gave reassurance to the woman, but she couldn't stop crying. After a while, the black-haired woman slowly knelt in front of the woman. She went to put her hand on the woman's knee before hesitating and pulling back. She waited patiently for the woman to calm down before saying, "I'm pregnant too."

The woman looked up with tear-stained red eyes, wiping them clear and sniffling before asking, "You-you are?"

The black-haired woman nodded, reaching for the man's hand, who came and took it, sitting beside her. "My husband and I weren't expecting to have a baby, I thought I wouldn't get pregnant."

"But when you serve God, your plans can change in an instant." He squeezed his wife's hand.

"God?" asked the woman. "Don't tell me you're all some religious freaks?"

"We're not freaks, I'll promise you that," said the husband, chuckling.

"The Bible tells us that God knit us in our mother's womb. That he knew us before we were even born. Therefore, life begins at conception. So, your baby is alive right now. It may just be a clump of cells with no form or distinguishing features. But think of us, we're just a clump of cells as well, whether you're a day old or ninety years old."

"So....so you're not going to take my baby away?" asked the woman, staring into the wife's eyes.

"No," replied the wife. "We would never harm a child." The wife reached her hand out again and gently laid it on the woman's knee, who immediately began crying, not out of fear but out of relief.

The brown-haired woman scooted in next to the woman who leaned over, crying into her shoulder. The brown-haired woman wrapped her arms around the woman for a long time.

When she could finally speak again, the woman said, "Thank you."

"Of course." The brown-haired woman pulled her arms tighter around the woman.

"I'm sorry for overreacting," said the woman, sitting up and wiping her nose on her shirt.

"No need to apologize," said the husband, standing up. "Let's get you cleaned up." He offered a hand and pulled the woman up.

After some time in the bathroom, the woman came back

freshened up, her eyes still slightly red.

"Feel better?" asked the wife.

"Much better," replied the woman, sitting on the bed. "I did have a couple of questions though, if you don't mind?" she asked, looking at the husband.

"Shoot."

"Is this dream that you had of me, is that from God?"

"I believe it is," said the husband with full confidence.

The woman nodded her head. "And when you came to the restroom, you believe that promoting was from God?"

"Yes," said the brown-haired woman.

The woman scratched her head. "Hmm... That's a lot to process."

"You don't have to understand today," said the brown-haired woman, "and neither do we expect you to understand today."

"Trust me," said the husband, "even I still don't understand it all."

The woman contemplated everything on her mind, and when at a loss for what to ask, simply said, "Where do we go from here?"

Everyone was silent a moment before the brown-haired woman said, "I've been thinking about that too." She got up and pulled out a sweater from the closet. "I've lost a little weight since I've been here, but this looks like it should fit you without causing any suspicion." She handed the sweater to the woman. "It should hide your stomach for a while once you begin to show more."

The woman tried on the loose sweater, not looking out of place on her. She spun around making sure the sweater looked appropriate from all angles.

"It's perfect," said the wife.

"I agree," said the husband.

"It won't last forever though," said the brown-haired woman, crossing her arms.

The Nameless Woman

"That's not today though," said the wife. "We'll deal with that when we get there."

"Yes... you're right." The brown-haired woman put her hands on her hips. "Why don't we pray together and send you off. I don't think it's smart to keep you here overnight. We can do that later once we've had more time together and security won't suspect anything."

"I agree," said the husband, standing. "Let's pray."

"Pray?" asked the woman. "I've never prayed before, nor am I a Christian."

"Don't worry," said the husband, "just listen." He began praying, bowing his head as his wife and brown-haired woman did the same. The woman just stared at them a moment before bowing her head out of respect.

The woman listened to the prayer, hearing the man passionately pray for safety, protection, wisdom, and knowledge. They even prayed for protection for her baby. The woman was very appreciative of the prayers but didn't believe any of them would work. A plan with a lot of luck was the only thing going to get her out of this situation. The only thing that still didn't make sense was how the husband had a dream about her when they had never met before.

She had heard many times you could only have dreams of people you've met before. So, was that not true, or had they actually met before? Maybe a passing glance, or a bump in at a coffee shop. There had to be a logical reason the husband had a dream about her. But that then didn't explain the prompting to go to the bathroom from the brown-haired woman. The woman's head began to spin when someone shook her arm.

"Are you ok?" asked the brown-haired woman.

"Yeah, yeah," said the woman. I was just thinking."

"About what?" asked the wife.

"About everything."

"Do you have a notebook?" asked the husband.

"No."

The husband dug through his closet, finding a blue journal that he opened, signed, and handed to the woman. She immediately turned to find what the husband had signed. "So you don't go crazy with everything happening to you. We're here for you whatever questions you have."

"Thank you," said the woman, closing the journal.

"Whatever you need we're here for you."

"We're not going to let them hurt our children," said the wife, putting a hand on her stomach.

The woman just nodded her head.

"I think it's time for you to decompress," said the brown-haired woman, guiding the woman to the door. "Let's meet for breakfast tomorrow. Does eight thirty work?"

"Yeah, that should work."

"Perfect. Enjoy the rest of your evening."

"I will. You do the same."

"You'll need your watch," said the husband, heading to a closet.

"Why did you take it?" asked the woman.

The husband had opened the closet door but stopped and closed it. "Out of precaution for listening devices. I've done all I can to our monitor, and the watches we hide in our bags."

"Do you think they heard this conversation?" asked the woman.

"I'm praying they didn't."

The room was silent a while before the woman said, "I guess we'll find out pretty quickly if they did."

"Let's hope that doesn't happen," said the brown-haired woman.

"You're right," said the wife. "And if something does happen, we'll do everything we can to help you."

"Just be careful what you say around your watch and any of the monitors," said the husband.

The woman didn't know how to respond. She had never experienced this kind of care and kindness from complete strangers. She simply nodded and said, "Thank you."

"Now it's time for you to go," said the husband, handing the woman her watch back.

Everyone waved as the woman left. Walking down the hall, the woman had a renewed sense that her baby might actually survive, making her grin.

***

As the door slid shut, everyone inside the room was frozen. For a long time, no one moved.

"Do you think it worked?" the brown-haired woman finally asked.

"If not," said the wife, "we'll need to pray very hard."

"I'm confident they didn't hear us," said the husband, thinking back through all the steps he took to ensure the monitor wasn't able to hear or see their previous conversation. "The real question is, if someone did hear us, how long until they act against us?"

11

As the woman opened the door to the hallway where her room was, a small crowd of people had gathered just inside. She hugged the back of the crowd looking through to find a group of what appeared to be security personnel assembling in front of a door. They wore all black with helmets, body armor, and guns. Another of these security guards stood in front of some barricades that spanned the length of the hallway.

"Open the door or we'll force our way in!" yelled one of the security personnel near the door. If there was a conversation happening, the woman couldn't hear it.

"Open the door or we'll force our way in!" yelled the same security personnel. "You have five seconds to comply!" After a moment, he motioned to one of the other personnel who walked up to the door monitor, holding out a card just in front of it. The rest of the group fanned out away from the door, all raising their guns toward the door.

The woman was counting in her head and a moment after she counted five seconds, the personnel scanned the card to the door monitor. He tried it again but clearly something was wrong when everyone scrambled around. One of the personnel carried a long tube with handles, a point on one end and a flat end on the other. Swinging it back, he rammed the flat end multiple times into the door before switching to the pointed end. After several hits, he stepped back as two personnel grabbed onto the door and began pulling it open. A chorus of orders and screams came from all the personnel as they waited for the door to be fully opened, charging through the second it was.

A woman's screams came from inside the room, echoing down the hall. Clearly a struggle was occurring by all the yelling and banging. And in less than a minute, a woman was dragged out of the room. Two personnel dragged her backwards by her arms as she screamed, "You killed my husband! You killed my husband!" She squirmed and fought trying to escape her captors' grasps as tears streamed down her face.

"Everybody, back against the wall!" yelled the personnel standing in front of the crowd, picking up a barrier and directing the group where to move. The crowd was crammed against one side of the hallway, the barrier sat in front of them as the woman from the room was dragged past. The woman's heart leapt into her mouth when she saw the woman being dragged past was pregnant.

She glanced down at her stomach, hoping no one could see her bump. The pregnant woman's bloodcurdling screams continued even after she was out of sight from the crowd in the hallway. It sent a shiver down the woman's spine as she was stuck in the back of the crowd, unable to move and forced to endure the woman's screams.

Another shiver went down her spine when the security personnel filed out of the hallway. Their boots all stomping in unison on their way past. Two of the personnel picked up the barricades as they passed, and with that, everyone was gone, like nothing had even happened.

Everyone from the group cautiously looked around before making their way down to the door that was broken into. It was closed, but a part of the door panel had been dented enough to make a hand hold. No one dared touch the door, but no one knew what else to do, so the group lingered a while and slowly dispersed, murmurs dotting the groups that left.

The woman hurried away from the crowd with the first few that left. Entering her room, she leaned back against her door, closed her eyes, took a deep breath, and clutched her notebook to her chest.

After a moment the woman realized she wasn't crying, something she probably would have done had she experienced the pregnant woman be dragged from her room just yesterday. But today, there was a hope she didn't have before. A hope from, she guessed she could call them friends now, the friends that would help her have her baby.

The woman put her hand over her stomach, rubbing her bump. Instead of whispering "I'll do my best to carry you to term," she said with confidence, "I will carry you to term."

PART 3: SECOND TRIMESTER

12

Over the following weeks, the woman began to grow closer with her new friends who were helping fight for her baby. They would sit together for every meal, simply giving the illusion that the group was just friends and nothing more. The woman had grown to like her new friends more than she was expecting. Then in the confines of the brown-haired woman's room, with the monitor disabled and watches hidden in the closet, everyone would share their findings of the day. Everything from where security personnel were stationed, locations of monitors, specific people seen every day that could be following them, and any "takings" as the ship's passengers started calling them, when security personnel would take a pregnant woman and abort her baby. It was to the point now where everyone, even the woman, had become numb to them.

One morning at breakfast, the woman and wife now showing considerable bumps but still managing to hide them, the group heard a commotion begin in one of the food lines. Everyone stopped and looked toward a man yelling murderer, pointing at a woman and what appeared to be her husband and two kids. The family didn't say anything and continued on until the man stopped in front of them. "She's trying to carry her child to term," he yelled for everyone to hear. "Look at her stomach!"

At first, the woman couldn't see that this woman was pregnant. But as the family turned around, it was clear that even with all the clothes she wore, this woman was pregnant.

"Murderer!" yelled a woman.

"Murderer!" Yelled a man, joining her.

And before long the entire cafeteria was filled with the chanting, "Murderer, murderer, murderer!" Whether people weren't chanting was impossible to tell. The woman and her group, however, had their mouths firmly shut, every one of them trying to hide the horrified expression on their face.

There had never been security personnel in the cafeteria, but there were always patrols that could get there at a moment's notice. The woman noticed several flight attendants pressing their watches. It was just a matter of time before that mother would be swept away, and the woman couldn't do anything to help.

In every other taking, everyone would simply crumple to the floor. They knew there was nowhere to run, nowhere to hide. They were on a ship in the middle of space, no one was going anywhere. This family, however, had a spark of defiance in their eyes. They frantically looked around as the husband grabbed his wife's hand, running toward the door to the garden.

The whole room was frozen for several seconds, stunned at the events unfolding in front of them. But in an instant, the fog cleared from everyone. One man jumped up to intercept the wife, missing and landing face first on the ground. The children jumped over the man, continuing to race after their parents. A group from one of the tables jumped up, making a wall that the kids slammed into, being caught a moment later.

"Dad!" screamed the boy.

"Help!" screamed the girl, reaching for her brother's hand. The father looked back at his kids, despair in his eyes just as his wife was snatched away from him. He punched his wife's captor in the face, pulling her away as the whole cafeteria stood, uproars of yelling, screaming, and running.

The woman looked on in sheer terror as the family was quickly overwhelmed. Their screams drowned out in the chaos of everything. The woman grabbed the wife's hand, staring in complete shock as the two held each other's hand under the table. The husband came behind them putting his arm on both their shoulders.

Even with all the noise, the woman could hear the wife's prayers, something the woman thought seemed pointless at this point. There was now a mob around the family. From their distance, the woman couldn't see anything that was happening.

The garden door opened, and the black suits of the police personnel caught the woman's eye. They rushed toward the crowd, pushing and shoving their way through, making slow progress but eventually reaching the center. They formed a circle, presumably around the family, and a moment later, pulled all four of them to their feet.

Even among the noise of the crowd, gasps and shrieks rose above. The woman and the wife both covered their mouths when they saw the state of the family. The father was nearly unrecognizable; blood and bruises covered his entire face. His wife was in a similar state, though if there was any damage to her womb, it wasn't visible. And the kids...

It made the woman's stomach churn, and the wife let go of her hand to puke behind them. The husband immediately held his wife's hair up and rubbed a hand on her back.

This was wrong. The woman knew it was wrong, but there was nothing anyone could do about it.

The security personnel pushed a path through the crowd, dragging the family out. Not one of them put up a fight, tried to get away, or resisted in any way. They dragged them back to the garden doors, all the security personnel crammed inside but two, who stayed behind guarding the door after it closed.

The room broke out in a deafening applause that lasted a very long time. So long in fact that the room began to smell of vomit; clearly the wife wasn't the only one who had thrown up.

As the smell wafted further from its sources, the noise began to die down, and people slowly scattered from the room.

The Nameless Woman

"Let's get out of here," said the husband, ensuring he walked in front of his wife and the woman, doing his best to hide their bumps.

They walked out in a small crowd, able to blend in as they came outside. "Let's head back to my place," said the brown-haired woman, leading the way. On their way to her room, the group passed one of the multiple medical facilities on the ship. This one had a line stretching down the hall of at least twenty women. A sign on the floor near the entrance read, "You're baby's life or the death of the human race?" Another piece of propaganda.

"They probably flocked there after the demonstration in the cafeteria," said the husband in a hushed tone.

"That's what fear does to people," said the wife. The rest of the way back to their room the group was silent. As soon as they entered, all the precautions were taken so they couldn't be heard, and there was a collective sigh as everyone could speak freely.

"This is getting scary," said the wife. "They've turned the whole ship against us."

"That's what the propaganda is designed to do," said the brown-haired woman.

"It's just signs though?" asked the woman.

"It's the bombardment of these signs everywhere you go," said the wife.

"As well the demonstrations of those signs being put into practice," said the husband. "Remember the first taking compared to this one? Everyone has become numb to them."

Everyone was silent as that thought sunk in.

"This is the third taking this week," said the woman, laying down on the bed with her hands over her face. "How long can we keep this a secret?"

No one replied.

"If someone sees us," continued the woman, "in any of the crowded areas of the ship... We'll turn out just like that family."

No one could look at each other. Everyone was distant, their fears and doubts clouding their minds. Finally, the brown-haired woman spoke up, "We need a new plan."

"Like what?" asked the wife.

"How do we get you two food without you going in the cafeteria?"

"We can't play the sick card," said the husband. "I've heard stories of people getting a little sick and immediately being quarantined by the medical staff. They'll find out immediately."

"What about the spare food table?" asked the woman, sitting up.

"There's a flight attendant always guarding it," said the wife. "As well as all the doors. I saw someone try to leave with their dessert, and you would have thought he was an Infected by the chaos that caused."

The brown-haired woman sighed. "It's like they want to draw us out."

"Everyone needs to eat," said the husband. "And with them tracking your eating, they make sure everyone gets their food. Just like what you said happened after the first taking," the husband looked toward the woman, "they forced their way into your room after you weren't scanning food out."

A defeated silence filled the room. There was very little hope in anyone's eyes.

"Then let's pray," said the brown-haired woman.

"With all due respect," said the woman, "look at what prayer has gotten us so far."

"Sometimes that's the case," said the husband.

"Then why do it?"

"Because we have faith," said the brown-haired woman.

"Well, I'm having very little faith that either of us are going to have our babies now." The woman got up, ensuring her sweater covered up her stomach. "You all can see the writing on the wall, our situation is hopeless." A tear ran down the woman's face. "There's no way we're going to survive this."

The Nameless Woman

The woman looked down at her stomach, rubbing a hand over it as tears fell from her face.

The wife walked up to the woman, wiping away her tears. "We're going to get out of this. We didn't come all this way just to give up."

"There's nothing we can do though," said the woman through more tears. "Someone's going to find out, or we're going to have to hide, and they'll eventually come looking for us. There's nowhere to go on this ship. We're stuck here on this death trap!"

"Calm down." The wife wrapped her arms around the woman's shoulders. "It may look grim now, but I have faith God will see us through and let us have our babies."

The woman stood there with tears continuing to stream down her face. "I need to go. I can't be with you anymore. I'm putting you all in danger."

"You can't lose hope now," said the brown-haired woman. "We don't know what tomorrow—

"You're better off without me." The woman spun around and rushed out of the room. Everyone inside cried out to her as she left, not wanting her to leave.

The woman started running down the hall, clutching her stomach before her instincts kicked in that had been drilled into her over the last few weeks. Don't run, don't do anything that would draw attention to yourself, and don't hold your stomach. She walked as fast as she could back to her room, keeping her head down so no one could see her tear-stained eyes.

Not many people were out and about this early in the evening, so the woman made it back to her room without any odd looks or questions that she knew of, only looking at the ground.

She jumped in her bed, pulling the covers up over her head. Again, her instincts kicked in, and she didn't say anything in front of her monitor or her watch. She realized though, she didn't feel the watch. Rubbing her wrist in the dark, she found her watch gone. She must have left it in the brown-haired woman's room.

Despite the impulse to speak her mind, she couldn't stand if the monitor heard her rambling and caused her baby never to see the light of day. She wasn't going to go down without fighting. So, she let her tears speak for her, crying herself to sleep once again.

Just as the woman walked up to the brown-haired woman's door, it slid open. Both women were frozen as they stared at each other, a million thoughts going through each of their heads.

"I'm glad your back," said the brown-haired woman. "I didn't know if you'd be back or not."

"Well... I actually just came back for my watch." The woman looked away as she rubbed the back of her head.

"Oh... I'll go get that for you." The brown-haired woman suntered back into the room, coming back out with the watch in hand. Before handing it to the woman, she asked, "Will you come back?"

The woman contemplated her answer before grabbing the watch, ensuring to wrap her hands fully around it so it couldn't hear her reply. "I don't know," she whispered. "Thinking last night... I don't want to put any of you in danger if I'm caught. I couldn't live with myself if that happened."

"We took that risk when we first brought you in," whispered the brown-haired woman. "You don't need to feel guilty for what others will do to us."

A tear ran down the woman's face, and she looked away. "I can't do that to you," she whispered, taking the watch and walking away. The brown-haired woman's hand reached out as the woman walked away. No rebuttal came from her mouth as she didn't know what to say, completely heartbroken.

E.E. Cooley

The woman strapped her watch back on, wiping the tears from her face as quickly as she could. Walking past the cafeteria, she hesitated, debating if it was worth the risk to eat food. Her watch read 9:30, easily the busiest time for breakfast as the research her and her now ex-friends showed. She could slip into the crowd and get out hopefully without being noticed.

As the doors opened, just as she predicted, the room was packed. Quickly getting in one of the longer lines, she got her food and sat down without any trouble. The woman could feel her heart beating in her ears as she ate, eyes darting all around, until she thought that looked too suspicious. Every eye that crossed her path made her heart skip a beat. She instinctively held her stomach with one hand under the table. No one was going to take her baby.

Near the end of her meal, the woman glanced to the food lines, finding the brown-haired woman in line with the husband and wife. They were all talking to the cafeteria employee when the wife rubbed a hand over her stomach before hiding it with a scratch. The employee didn't seem to notice, from what the woman though at least.

The woman's hands started to sweat as the interaction continued for longer than what she thought was normal. Then the group finally left the line. Security didn't rush in, and none of their faces looked scared out of their minds; in fact, they looked joyful. She quickly looked away, not wanting them to notice her, but a moment later, they found her. "What are you doing here?" she whispered angrily to them. "Are you ok?" she asked a little calmer.

"We're ok," said the wife. She moved her spoon from the side to the top of her plate, laying it parallel to the top of the tray. This indicated something needed to be said but away from prying ears and monitors. The majority of the time that meant everyone would go back to the brown-haired woman's room to discuss the matter, but this time was different.

Everyone acted like they were best friends, laughing and

talking like any group would; however, the woman was noticeably absent from much of the conversation. Unsure how to act after the last conversation she had with the brown-haired woman.

They talked longer than normal, everyone having finished their food long ago when they finally got up to leave. Everyone had been glancing back toward the employee they'd talked to in line. He left the line, and a minute later, everyone got up to leave. The woman followed them as they put up their trays, exiting through the garden. She wasn't sure why she followed, whether it was instinct, guilt, or the fact that she didn't really want to be alone. That doing something was better than hiding in her room all day

Entering the garden was a nice change of color from the drab walls of the ship. It also smelled much better. The woman always regretted not coming in here more as it always renewed her energy and spirits. When she got to the clearing, however, she remembered why she didn't come back more often. Seeing the empty stage brought back too many memories of that horrible day on the ship.

The woman desperately wanted to ask where they were going, but everyone knew not to ask questions in public that if heard could reveal their secret. So they walked across the clearing, taking one of the many paths that converged at the door out of the garden. In the middle of their path, a man leaned against a tree, his arms crossed and head bowed, just off the path. He looked up at the group at the sound of their footsteps and stepped away from the tree, greeting then with a grin. He put his finger over his lips and held out an open bag. Pointing to his watch, everyone took their watches off, putting them inside the bag. When the bag was shut, the man said, "I'm glad you came."

"I immediately trusted you," said the husband. "I wouldn't have come if I didn't."

"Good, follow me." The man waved them off the path and

into the trees, stopping well off the path that you'd have to be deliberately looking to see the group.

"We'll make this quick," said the man. "I could tell you were pregnant today in line." He looked toward the wife. "Which means others will notice too. But I'm not turning you in." The woman breathed out a breath she didn't realize she had been holding.

"I've seen what happens after the takings." It looked like the man was reliving a nightmare in his eyes as he paused. "It's horrendous," he finally said. "I don't want that to happen to you. So I have a plan. I always walk through the garden after my shift. It ends at 10:30 in the morning and 4 in the afternoon. I can sneak food out to one of you who will be waiting along this path. I'll pass the food off to you and that way you'll be able to stay in your room." The man looked at the wife again. "I'll always bring a little extra so you can start to stockpile food. I could lose my job or be found out about this, so I'd like it if you were prepared for that."

"What about our watches tracking when we check out food?" asked the woman. "They'll see that we're not getting any food?"

"Don't worry, I can input your watches into our system and make it look like you signed out food. Trust me, I'll make sure you can stay hidden."

"And you're not going to sell us out?" asked the brown-haired woman.

"No. I would never do that. I can't stand to see another baby killed on this ship. Or another mother's cries echo through the ship as she's dragged away." A lone tear rolled down the man's face before he looked away, wiping his face. There was a genuineness the woman found in the man, one only her other friends back on Earth had displayed.

"I trust him," said the woman, taken aback she had spoken her thoughts. Everyone else shared her agreement, making the man smile.

"I promise your baby will be born," he said, looking the wife in the eyes, and then everyone else.

"So what's the plan then?" asked the husband.

So the group discussed the plan. Setting times for the man to drop food off, things to be careful about, and everything the man thought would be necessary to convey to the group.

As the conversation neared the end, the woman realized they had only discussed plans about the wife's baby, not hers. "Excuse me," she said when there was a slight pause in the conversation.

"Yes," said the man.

"I, uh," the woman put a hand on the back of her head, "I thought you should know that I'm pregnant too."

"Oh," said the man taken aback. "That's wonderful," he said with a smile. "That shouldn't complicate things too much. You said you have a two bedroom room correct?" He asked, looking at the wife.

"Correct."

"That's perfect, you two can just stay in the back room together. I'll bring a little extra food, and you just hunker down until you have your babies."

Then a question jumped to the front of the woman's mind that made her feel stupid for not seeing it earlier. "What about using the restroom? We can't go out to use the public restroom once we really start to show?"

Everyone looked genuinely stunned they hadn't considered this. Questions raced across their minds when the man asked, "Is your room on the same side of the hall or the opposite side as your bathroom?"

"The same side," said the husband.

"I might have an idea. I'll do some investigating and get back with you. "The man suddenly looked behind himself. "But we've been here too long. We need to get going."

"Thank you for your help," said the woman, feeling relieved after what felt like a brick of despair had been dropped on her. Everyone else said their thanks and the group dispersed, heading back to their respective rooms.

The walk back to the brown-haired woman's room was much lighter this time, everyone was filled with a renewed hope, especially the woman. After all their watches were off and put away in the room, there was a collective sigh and celebration.

When everything died down, the woman said, "I'm sorry for leaving you guys. I'm sorry I thought being away from you would make you safer. I should have trusted you more." Not a tear fell from her face, but the guilt was immense. She couldn't look anyone in the eye, she didn't even know if they were still her friends.

The brown-haired woman walked up, putting her hands on the woman's shoulders. "We're glad you're back," was all she said with a smile.

The woman was confused at the response, and when she couldn't shake it, asked, "That's it? No rebuttal, no lesson, just welcome back. After I left you guys—"

"Yes. It's that simple." The brown-haired woman squeezed the woman's shoulders.

"It can't be that simple," pleaded the woman.

"It is," said the wife, walking up and putting her hand on the woman's arm.

"I don't understand?" asked the woman.

"It's just like the story of the prodigal son," said the husband. "Have you heard this story?"

The woman shook her head.

"A son decides to take his father's inheritance and leave. He goes into the town and ends up blowing all his money. With nothing left, the son returns to his father, who welcomes his son home with open arms, despite everything he did."

"Why did the father do that?"

"Because he loves his son."

"But I'm not your son?"

"It doesn't matter," said the brown-haired woman. "We love you just the same."

Something she had never felt before washed over the woman like a wave. A peace unlike anything she had known consumed her. She cried, for the first time since being on the ship, out of joy. There was no fear in these tears. Everyone surrounded the woman, hugging her for long after she stopped crying.

When they pulled apart, there was a renewed strength and energy to everyone. Smiles spread across faces and spirits were lifted. This was not going to be the end for their children. Their hope had been restored.

14

The next morning the woman woke up in the brown-haired woman's room, getting the best night sleep she had since being on the ship. It was a relief to finally wake up well-rested and recharged. It wasn't long before the rest of the room was up.

"Alright," said the husband. "The employee said he'd be in the garden in about forty-five minutes. We'll go get our breakfast and come back with yours."

"Sounds good," said the wife. Everyone waved bye as the husband and brown-haired woman left. As soon as the door closed, the wife said, "I really need to use the restroom."

"I do too." The woman put a hand over to stomach. "How are you going to go out there without being seen?"

"Well what time is it," the wife asked, looking at the monitor in the main room. "It's the busiest time for breakfast now, so if we go out now, we probably won't run into anyone."

"But the camera's will see you?"

The wife got up and looked through all the closets until she found a coat. "This should cover it."

"Good idea." The woman helped the wife put the coat on, and they confidently walked to the bathroom just a few doors down. No one was in the hallway, and as they entered the bathroom, both women breathed a sigh of relief, finding no one inside.

"Let's make this quick," said the wife, taking a stall, and a few minutes later, they were out, back in their room with no

The Nameless Woman

hassle, both falling on the couch in exhaustion.

"I never thought using the restroom would be that stressful," said the woman between breaths.

"Me neither," said the wife. They both laid on the bed for several minutes, feeling like they had just finished running a marathon.

"We can't lay here forever," said the wife, sitting up. "We need to do something."

"I can work out," said the woman. "Or at least stretch for the day."

I'm going to read my Bible," said the wife. "I'll head in the bedroom so I can concentrate." She pulled her Bible out of a closet and headed to the extra bedroom, sliding the door shut behind her.

The woman changed out of her pajamas, pushed the bed up into the wall, and began working out. The last time she had done any exercise of any kind was back on Earth. She knew she wouldn't be as fit as she was then, but she realized that she was getting worn out very quickly. Not only that but some of her stretches she was unable to do now that she had a baby. And the same was true with the workouts she did.

Eventually after not being able to do as much as she wanted and being completely worn out, she pulled the bed back down, flopping on it but catching herself before her stomach hit the bed. And before she knew, it she fell asleep. An hour later she woke to the wife shaking her arm.

"I take it you found out how hard it is to work out?" asked the wife.

"Yeah," said the woman, rubbing the sleep from her eyes and sitting up. "I didn't think it would wear me out that much." The door opened behind them as the husband and the brown-haired woman stepped through. As soon as the door closed and they had put up their watches, the husband said, "We come bearing gifts," holding up a small crate.

"Perfect timing," said the woman.

"What is that," asked the wife.

"This is how your food will be transported. We'll exchange it each time for a different crate with new food. This was the only way that man said we could move food around the ship without being suspicious." The husband handed out the food, packaged in reusable containers, to his wife and the woman. They both thanked the husband and began eating.

The husband brought the crate into the spare bedroom without a word and began pulling tools out.

"Where did you get those?" asked the wife, staring into the room.

"This is supposed to solve the bathroom problem," said the husband as he began taking apart the floor next to the bed.

"How is taking the floor apart supposed to do that?" asked the woman.

"This should give us access to the sewage running from the bathrooms." The husband managed to loosen the floor plate and removed it entirely. Looking inside, he froze as a smile broke out across his face, and he chuckled.

"What is it?" asked the wife.

"It's a miracle," said the husband. "There's a hookup to the pipe from here. It's like this room was meant to have a toilet in it."

The brown-haired woman walked over to the hole in the floor, leaning over to look inside. A similar smile broke across her face. "God certainly has his hand on us."

"Yes, He does," said the husband.

The atmosphere in the room genuinely changed at that moment. There was a hopefulness unlike any before, and it only grew.

Over the following days, supplies were snuck into the brown-haired woman's room to create a bare-bones toilet for the wife and woman to use. It was able to be torn down so the floor could be put back in place; in the event of a search, no one would know it was there.

The Nameless Woman

As soon as the toilet was completed, a burden felt as if it was lifted from the woman. A peace filled everyone knowing that their situation had drastically improved. All that was on everyone's mind was to get these babies to term.

As the days passed, everyone's confidence grew that this plan was going to work. Food was delivered and exchanged, the secret bathroom worked far better than anyone thought, and no one from the ship ever brought any suspicion or questions against the group.

Being stuck in their room all day meant the wife and the woman became close friends very quickly, by circumstance but also because they genuinely got along. The woman even began asking questions about the Bible. So the wife would take days to answer her questions, other days she would read from the Bible, and other days the two would discuss topics late into the night.

It was still a lot to take in for the woman. A lot of it didn't make sense, but she was slowly starting to understand why her new friends had shown her so much love and help to begin with. And it was from this love that the group became close knit. Their relationship with each other grew stronger and stronger every day.

Nights would be reserved for games, from the most simple to the most complex they could come up with; anything they could do to entertain themselves.

Despite the continued takings, despite the fear that lingered in the far recesses of everyone's minds, there was a hope and confidence that overshadowed it all. So much so that the woman noticed she couldn't remember the last time she had cried herself to sleep.

PART 4: THIRD TRIMESTER

The woman laid in her bed as she rubbed her stomach, her bump now substantial in size. It was impossible for either her or the wife to leave their room without anyone recognizing they were pregnant.

By this point, the woman and the wife couldn't remember how many days they had been confined to their room. The days began to blend together or feel like an eternity as insanity began to creep into the edges of the women's minds.

"I hate this," said the woman.

"What's that?" asked the wife, walking another lap around the bedroom.

"I can barely do anything anymore. I can hardly walk."

"Neither can I," said the wife between breaths. "But if I don't do this, I'll go crazy."

"I think you just have too much energy." The woman began laughing.

"What are you laughing at?" asked the wife, laughing along. They both fed off each other's laughter until the wife had to sit down on the bed.

"Oh goodness," said the wife with a sigh when they finally calmed down.

"We're definitely going crazy," said the woman with a chuckle before looking at the closed door. "They've been gone a while," she said, referring to the husband and brown-haired woman.

The Nameless Woman

"Maybe when we get our food, we won't be so crazy," said the wife.

The door flew open as the police personnel rushed into the room. "Hands in the air," yelled one of them as six entered the room, guns raised at the women, who were in complete shock they didn't even move. Two of the personnel handcuffed the women behind their backs, both of them putting up a fight that was useless. They began screaming for help as they were dragged out of the room.

As the police pulled them out of their room, the hallway was full of onlookers and gawkers, some staring out their rooms and others in groups behind barricades. As soon as they laid eyes on the women, they immediately began screaming and yelling, calling them murderers, liars, and all sorts of curses and slurs. The women continued to scream for help to no avail, no one was risking their safety to help these women, that is if anyone even wanted to help in the first place.

The wife stopped yelling and focused her energy on trying to escape the police, but it was no use. Their grips were too strong, and she was too weak.

The walk down the hallway felt like an eternity to the woman. Hearing the word murderer shouted over and over again at her. It was a lie, she didn't want to kill anyone, she just wanted to have her baby. But clearly no one else saw it that way. Or if they did, their voice was drowned out by the crowd. She wouldn't even put it past the crew of the ship to rat those dissenters out.

By the end of the hallway, the woman was a wreck. She had given up trying to escape and was balling, unable to control her tears. The crowd laughed at her when they saw her tears, beginning another slew of name-calling. And by the time they exited the hallway, both women were completely humiliated, distraught, overwhelmed, and completely defeated...

16

The women were taken down a cargo elevator near the back of the ship. Twelve police personnel filled the car, and neither woman could see what floor was selected. The doors opened, and everyone was hit with a rush of heat. The woman closed her eyes as she was shoved out, immediately hit with a blast of cool air in her back from a fan above the door, only to be swarmed by the heat of the room once again.

They were escorted down narrow hallways with minimal lighting, and as they rounded a corner, the woman could make out screams in the distance. There was an old style prison door made with rods of metal that they passed through before coming to a wide open room. The source of the heat was clear as a giant incinerator sat against the far wall of the room. They continued through to a hallway opposite them. The further they got into the room, the more it stunk. The woman was so distraught though that she couldn't think of what the smell was, only that it was overwhelming.

A long conveyor belt fed into the incinerator with people working on both sides, throwing items from carts onto the conveyor. Tubes in the ceiling dropped items into containers that workers shifted through as well. There was so much to take in. It was too much for the woman to remember everything.

The screams started to become louder as they reached the other side of the room, taking a hallway away from the incinerator room. Several hallways branched off to the right;

The Nameless Woman

the wife was dragged through the third of these branching paths, but not without protests from the woman.

When they finally dragged the two away, the screams were overwhelming from the echoes, they were coming from within these halls. The thought sent a chill down the woman's spine as she was dragged to a further branch.

The branches were lined with prison cells on both sides, using the same old style prison doors as when they first entered. The police took her to a cell near the end of the hallway and shoved her inside, locking the door behind her.

Despite the heat in the room, the floor was cold, which was a relief to the woman as she curled up in a ball on the floor, clutching her stomach. For the first time she found herself thanking God that her baby hadn't been aborted yet. Which was a strange sensation for her that she was even doing this, but at the same time, it seemed the only thing she could do.

A scream from nearby broke her out of her thoughts as a woman's bloodcurdling screams echoed off the walls from somewhere nearby. The woman covered her ears, but they couldn't do enough. The scream was so demoralizing.

Eventually the woman had backed into a corner of the room, doing everything she could to block out the nightmare she found herself in.

Some time later the opening of her cell door jerked the woman's eyes open. The light from the hallway shadowed the three people who came in, making it impossible for the woman to figure out who they were.

The person in front walked over to the woman and squatted down, while the other two people stayed a few steps behind. "Hi there," said the woman, squatting in front of her. The woman could now make out that this woman was wearing a suit similar to the captain, as well as a cap with her hair done up in a tight bun. "My name is the Director," she said in a cheery voice but with a venom behind it. "Whenever I talk to you, you will reply with either 'yes Director' or 'no Director.'"

The woman just stared at the Director, not knowing what to say.

"Answer me!" barked the Director, making the woman flinched.

"What are you going to do—"

The Director slapped the woman across the face. Barely above a whisper, the Director said, "You only ask questions if I give you permission, understood?"

Everything in the woman didn't want to say it, but she knew she had too. "Yes, Director."

"Good girl." The Director ruffled the woman's hair like she was a dog. "Now about your child, or your womb, or your clump of cells, whatever you call what's inside your stomach, you have one option. Every day you will work the incinerator line. Pulling all our junk that we can't reuse and dump it onto the line. You'll do that until you can't keep up with your work, at which point you would have an abortion. That's what would normally happen.

"However, you and your murderous friend were hiding out for a very long time. You even destroyed property for your toilet, used a ship employee to smuggle food into your room, and did that for seven months. So instead, I have something else planned." The Director paused letting the words sink into the woman, who became increasingly agitated, not knowing what to do or if she should even move. But a scream broke out; the woman looked toward the door as the Director and the guards were unphased.

"That's actually what will happen to you," said the Director.

Instantly, a horrified look spread across the woman's face. She tried to ask what caused the scream, but her words were caught in her throat.

"Well as you know," began the Director, "we can't get each other pregnant on the ship. And for good reason, we don't want to compromise our food supply. If we do that, people could end

The Nameless Woman

up dying because someone has to choose who gets food and who doesn't. No one needs to be put in that situation.

"However, because of that, less people on the ship are having sex, out of fear they become a murderer, especially my guards here," the Director motioned behind her at the guards. "But now that so many of you are getting pregnant, we have a remedy for our sexless passengers."

The woman nearly paled as she connected the dots. "No..." she mumbled over and over.

"I see you're getting it," the Director said with a smirk. "Whenever our guards feel the need, they'll have sex with you whenever they want."

"That's not sex," the woman said, getting power back behind her voice. "That's rape!" she yelled.

"No, it's not," said the Director, looking genuinely confused. "Rape is unwanted or forced sex. You clearly wanted and had sex to get that murderous abomination in your stomach."

"It's not an abomination!" yelled the woman. "It's my child!"

"You can call it whatever you want." The Director held up her hands defensively. "These are just the consequences for your actions, which I don't even know why you see them as consequences. We're saving lives by doing this. We're saving the human race."

"You'll lose the human race trying to save it this way."

"No, we won't! You'll be the ones to destroy it!" yelled the Director, pointing a finger at the woman. She stood up, walked toward the door, and stopped just before exiting. "Because you're so pregnant," the Director said over her shoulder, "your abortion will be in a week."

Tears began pouring down the woman's face. "You're a monster."

"How am I a monster for wanting what's best for my troops!" the Director screamed. "You're the monster! You all are the monster, trying to murder us all! You don't want to see the human race live, you want to see it burn." An idea popped into the Director's head, and a grin broke out across her face. She resumed her calm and confident posture as when she first walked into the cell, flattening out her suit. "Don't worry," she said, exuding confidence and power, "my troops have had their fill for the day. You're safe for now." The Director turned on her heel, exiting the cell with the guards in tow.

As they locked the cell, the woman curled back into a ball, hugging herself as tight as she could while she cried uncontrollably.

17

The captain stood in the control room, looking over all the technicians, communications, and additional personnel working about. The stars stretched as far as the eye could see through the viewport, the twinkle of the stars always making the captain smile when he saw one.

The captain's wife walked up, standing by her husband's side. "It's beautiful, isn't it?"

The captain grabbed his wife's hand. "Yes, it is." Then turning to his wife, he added, "But not as beautiful as you or our boy will be."

The wife smiled as a communications officer piped up. "We just got word two pregnant women were caught in a raid. And it's been discovered they've been hiding out for the last seven months." There was a mixture of applause and murmurs at the noise, but the captain cut in over the noise, silencing everyone.

"This is a great day but also a difficult day for us. We should all be glad another murderous thief was caught. But it should also be a wake-up call that there are still these people who think they can hide from us. I will not see the destruction of the human race because some people are too selfish." The captain scanned the control room before continuing. "Let's do our best to help out our crew in finding these thieves and ensure we give our passengers the best stay of any Worldship." The control room broke out in applause and cheers from everyone, making the captain and his wife smile.

As the applause died down, everyone got back to work with a renewed energy. "A good speech as always," said the captain's wife, rubbing his back.

The captain was going to respond when he was interrupted by his assistant. "Captain, the Prison Director has asked to see you." She motioned to the control room entrance where the Prison Director stood.

"Excuse me," said the captain, gently squeezing his wife's arm. He followed the assistant to the back of the control room. "I see you decided to bring them in." The captain crossed his arms, keeping his voice low.

"We're confident they wouldn't lead us to anyone else," said the Director, equally as quiet. "There was no point in letting them steal more of our food."

"So how many did you get?"

"Two pregnant women, two conspirators, and one staffer who conspired as well. Interrogations so far indicate the group ends with these five."

"Five of them managed to evade the public's eye." The captain shook his head. "How many more do we have under surveillance?"

"Twenty-four right now, sir."

The captain just nodded his head. "None of them will have their babies," he whispered to himself.

After a minute when the captain was still stuck in his thoughts, the Director asked, "Captain?"

"What—" he asked, looking at the Director. "Oh yes, did you have a question?"

"I did, sir. I had a proposal for what to do with our most recent capture."

"Let me hear it."

The Director outlined her idea to the captain, whose smile grew with every passing minute. And at the end of the proposal, he simply said, "Do it."

18

The woman huddled in the corner of her cell, her arms covering her face. The tears from the previous week had stained her face. The memories from the past week ingrained in her memory, they never wanted to leave her thoughts. And when she heard the cell door open, she pulled herself into a ball, hugging her knees the best she could. As she braced for the horrific misery she was about to endure...it never came.

She was roughly picked up by two guards who drug her out of the cell. When her eyes saw the light of the hallway, the woman began to cry out of relief. But that relief was quickly squashed when she asked, "Where are you taking me?"

When the guards didn't answer, she knew immediately where she was going. She had lost track of the days. It couldn't have been time...

She pulled against the guards, finding strength she didn't realize she had. After having barely any food or water, she expected to have absolutely no energy. The guards were surprised by the woman's strength, but it wasn't enough to overpower their grips.

The woman began to scream as she was dragged further and further down the hall, past more and more cells, the majority of them occupied, everyone looking away as the woman was dragged past.

The woman's screams reached far above the others in the prison. And as they finally reached the end of the hallway, rounding the corning, arrived at a short dead-end hallway. On the left side of the hallway was a single double door and nothing else.

The woman's screams reached their peak and were completely cut off as the doors closed behind her.

19

The woman, naked, laid on the operating table after just throwing up, sobbing uncontrollably. When the tears finally stopped flowing enough for her to see, she sat up, finding the mutilated remains of her child on a silver tray beside the bed. She crawled off the table, falling to the ground but able to reach up on the table for the tray. Bringing it to the floor, she held her child in her hands for hours. No words, only screams and tears expressed her emotions. For hours on end her agony filled the room.

***

Two guards stormed through the door, stopping when they saw the woman laying beside the tray with her child's remains. The woman looked up at them with puffy eyes and pleaded saying, "Don't take me away from my child...please."

The guards hesitated a second more before walking forward and picking the woman up, who screamed and struggled her way back to her child. But the guards were stronger as one pulled her away, and the other cut the woman's clothes off. This didn't matter to the woman, she just wanted to be next to her child. As the guards pulled her out of the room, the woman reached her hands toward her child, screaming in protest, her last act of defiance.

When the doors to the operating room closed, the woman

dropped her hand, defeated, humiliated, destroyed, and heartbroken. Through fresh tears, she screamed, "I'm sorry!" Saying it over and over again until it was just a mumble.

The guards drug the woman through the hallways and to the entrance elevator, where the Director and more guards were waiting. The director had a cup of red liquid that she used to write the word "MURDERER" on the woman's chest and back. The liquid ran down the woman's body before drying. With a smug grin, the Director stepped back to admire her work before everyone got in the elevator. The woman was supported in the middle of the elevator with the guards and Director surrounding her. At this point the woman didn't know what emotion to express. She just stood there, more leaning against the guards who held her, emotionless.

The elevator door opened, and the woman was escorted to a set of double doors. The Director stopped and turned around to face the woman. "Smile for the cameras," she said with a smile as she walked backwards and opened the doors. A rush of noise overwhelmed the woman as the guards pushed the woman forward. When she saw the crowd lining both sides of the hallway, the woman lost all strength in her legs, forcing the guards to drag her.

There were boos and shouts from the crowd. People crying murderer, thief, disgusting, monster, and a myriad of names and slurs. Suddenly, the woman was very aware of her situation, no longer not caring about her condition. She was being paraded around the ship, naked, with murderer written on her. The embarrassment and shame nearly overwhelmed the woman as she began to cry again.

Every word the crowd said lodged itself in the woman's mind, repeating itself over and over again. A fresh wave of agony and shame hit her with each additional utterance of the words. The only thought that was able to break through the bombardment of the crowd was a question, was the God her friends prayed to, that she learned about, that was taught about,

The Nameless Woman

that her friends trusted wholeheartedly, that she even prayed to, was He even real?

After the eternity of agony that the woman was paraded through the ship, they arrived at the garden. Giant monitors rose above the stage in the center of the clearing, the woman's naked body plastered over every single one. She craned her head around to find a cameraman following her. The woman blushed as the guards escorted her onto the stage, dropping her on her knees in the center of the stage.

The crowd beyond the woman slowly began packing in like sardines. There were no chairs this time, so everyone was standing shoulder to shoulder. The woman tried covering herself with her hands when the guards pulled them down, handcuffing them behind her back. the crowd laughed and pointed at the woman during this, making her blush and look away. Their curses, rebukes, and attacks continued until the captain stepped onto the stage. The crowd was completely silent as he stepped up to the podium and spoke into the microphone.

"Seven months... seven months this woman and her thieving friends conspired against us, stole our food, and damaged our ship!" An uproar came from the crowd that took several minutes to calm down. "I am just as outraged as you are. But fear not, for this thief," the captain pointed at the woman, "will no longer bring a child onto this ship that will kill us!" Applause and cheers rang out in every corner of the room.

When the noise had finally died down, the captain continued. "But because this murderer evaded us for so long, hid from us, stole from us, from you, she can't be trusted to stay on this ship, can she?" The crowd screamed their agreement with the captain. "So, it's only fitting that this murderous thief die in the very place she thought she could escape from. Earth!"

The woman was stunned as the crowd exploded. Before too long they were all chanting "Earth, Earth, Earth!"

"She will not kill us!" shouted the captain as the crowd went hysterical. The chanting turned into, "kill her, kill her, kill her."

The captain knew there was no quieting the crowd down now. "We'll send her back to Earth to die!" he screamed. "We'll send her back to die with the Infected! She will be the example that no one is above the law, no one can fight back, and no one will stop the human race from surviving!"

The roar from the crowd was so loud it shook the floor. All the woman wanted to do was cover her ears, but the guards yanked her to her feet. Dragging her off the stage, they went through to the side door of the garden. The guards forming a circle around the woman as the crowd tried to enact vengeance on the woman themselves.

As they exited the garden, the ship looked deserted, everyone clearly had left to see the woman. The guards went back to the elevator they had arrived in with no trouble. Going up a few floors and exiting onto a very ornate floor, a far cry from the drab gray and white walls she was familiar with.

The fact that she was concerned about the design of the floor was odd to the woman. She had far greater things to be concerned about, and one of them was being answered.

The guards brought her to a door that slid up. Inside were a couple of seats, a control console, and a small window at the far end of the room. When she realized what the room was, she started kicking her legs away. "Looks like someone's afraid of flying," said the Director, walking up to a monitor next to the door.

"I'm not going in there," said the woman.

"Throw her in," said the Director. "Remove her cuffs first." The guards complied, and the woman frantically shoved and kicked when the handcuffs were off, trying everything to escape. The guards picked the woman up by her arms and legs, holding her horizontal to the ground. Swinging her back and forth to gain momentum, the guards counted down from three

The Nameless Woman

before throwing the screaming woman into the escape pod.

The woman landed with a thud on the cold metal floor and cried out. The guards all laughed as she scrambled up as quickly as her weakened body could carry her, but the door slid shut before she made it halfway. "No, please!" she pleaded, crawling to the small window on the door. "I don't know how to fly!"

The Director never looked at her as she punched in commands on the monitor and turned to leave. The guards continued laughing as they followed the Director.

The woman continued pleading, banging her fist against the window until everyone had left. She slumped to the floor crying, pulling her hands over her head. Nothing seemed to matter to her, not the stone-cold floor, that she was naked, or that she didn't know how to fly the escape pod, only that she no longer had her child. The pieces of them on the tray burned into her memory.

Then a beep came from the pod. The woman looked up, finding a blinking red light on the console. She crawled over finding a countdown below the light.

"Attention all passengers," said a female voice from the console. "Please make your way to the nearest seat. The escape pod is about to launch." The countdown read less than two minutes. The woman crawled to the nearest seat on the side of the pod and strapped herself in, crying the whole time. When she got strapped in, the woman pulled her legs to her chest, wrapped her arms around her legs, and nestled her head into her knees as she cried. The only thing she remembered was feeling the jerk as the escape pod launched away from the Worldship, making its way down to the surface of Earth; the passengers of the Worldship cheering the entire way as they watched the pod and the murderous woman inside leave them forever.

PART 5: BIRTH

20

A gentle breeze blew across the valley, sending the scents of the flowers and lake wafting to every corner. A man sat against a tree reading a book, a picnic blanket and food laid out next to him. This man didn't use to smile, but it had become a regular occurrence as it was today. The man had found peace, joy, and a purpose in a world where many would consider those traits unattainable.

Then a sound the man had never heard before cracked through the sky. He closed his book and stood up, searching the sky for the source of the sound. A flash a light caught the man's eye as he found a ship of some kind descending toward the surface. Rockets flared from the front to slow its descent. Then there was an explosion as parachutes jettisoned from the rear of the ship, and the rockets turned off. Birds and animals scattered away to the nearest hiding place.

The ship floated toward the surface, and the more it descended, the more the man realized it was going to land in the valley. From the trajectory, the man guessed it would land far in front of him, and he wasn't far off. The ship hit the ground with too much speed and drug across the bottom of the valley, cutting a deep gash in the ground. It quickly lost its speed and came to a stop a good distance from the man, who sat his book on the ground and sprinted toward the wreck.

He was out of breath by the time he approached the smoking heap of a ship, which upon first inspection appeared intact. The man leaned over on his knees, catching his breath before walking over to the ship. A blinking red light shone to the right of a small window on the back of the ship. The light was next to a small door, which was near the engines, still blazing red and radiating heat. The man hesitantly reached for the small door, yanking his hand away as it began to burn him. Shaking his hand, he bundled his shirt up in his hand and tried the door, only for his hand to nearly get burned again.

Getting an idea, the man ran back to his tree and grabbed the picnic blanket and his water. He poured the still cold water over the hatch, creating a cloud of steam, before using the blanket to open the door. Inside was a red button with some instructions next to it. Quickly reading through it, the man discovered the ship was an escape pod, the button activated explosives that would blow the door off, and there was a ten second delay before the explosives detonated. The man pressed the button with the blanket and ran out of the path the door would shoot off, dropping on his stomach facing the escape pod. The hatch blew, taking the parachutes with it, blasting far away from the pod, flipping end over end as it crashed into the ground.

Slowly getting up, the man hesitantly walked toward the pod when a life raft exploded from the door and began inflating, scaring the man and making him jerk. When the raft fully inflated, it stayed attached to the pod on one end, causing the other to pivot to the ground and create a ramp inside.

Checking the raft and finding it cool to the touch, the man climbed up the ramp, ensuring the door frame wasn't hot before climbing up. Inside he found a completely naked woman huddled on the floor in the fetal position. He immediately took the blanket and threw it over the woman. "Ma'am, ma'am," the man asked, shaking her.

"Oww..." The woman groaned, putting her hands on her head.

"Can you hear me," the man asked, rolling the woman over

onto her back, ensuring the blanket covered her.

"They killed them."

"Killed who?"

"My child," the woman began crying, "they killed my child!"

After that the man couldn't get anything else out of the woman, even when he told the woman, "I'm going to pick you up and get you some help," all the woman could do was cry. The man wrapped the blanket around the woman and carried her out of the escape pod, all the way back to his hidden home in the valley. On his way there, others from the hidden home ran out and helped the man and the woman.

21

The woman woke up with her head throbbing, immediately groaning as her hands clutched her head.

"Hi," said a man, groggily reaching out and putting a hand on the woman's shoulder. She jerked back from his touch, looking the man up and down.

"Where am I?" she asked.

"You're somewhere secret, but someplace safe," said the man.

"What's that supposed to mean?"

"It means no one is going to harm you."

"Harm me...." said the woman.

"When the doctors were checking you they found..." The man couldn't finish the sentence.

"You're not going to hurt me?" asked the woman with disbelief in her eyes.

"I would never hurt you. I was the one who saved you from your escape pod."

Then the memories started flooding back to the woman. Everything up to being launched out the escape pod, everything after that was lost to the woman. But that loss was insignificant compared to the loss of her child. And that made the woman cry again, shoving her head into her pillow.

The man reached his hand out but stopped, remembering how the woman had pulled away before. He slowly got up from his chair, muttering a prayer for the woman as he left the room.

For the next three weeks, the woman laid in her bed. Only getting up to use the restroom when her stomach began to hurt. Doctors and nurses visited her through the days to ensure she was recovering and helping her in any way they could. But the one who was always there was the man who pulled the woman from the escape pod. He was there every day, ensuring there was a familiar face she could recognize. And that familiarity was vital to the woman's recovery. Over the three weeks the man had built up a trust that no one else had with the woman. Allowing her to be vulnerable with someone, which was hard for her to do at this stage.

This ended up leading to the man forcing the woman to get out of bed and take walks with him. They started off slowly, walking the halls around her bedroom and back, getting her body back up to strength. And then the man took the woman on a tour of the secret place that no one would name.

"And this is my favorite room," said the man, walking into the chapel. There was an uneasiness to the woman as she took in the room, as was the case when anyone had come to her room and prayed over her the last three weeks. "We've had a lot of people pray for you in here," said the man with a smile.

"Well, they don't seem to be working yet," said the woman almost mockingly.

"After what you've been through, we don't expect you to be healed overnight. We would love a miracle, but we understand that you'll need a while to recover."

"And just how long will that be?" asked the woman to no one in particular.

"Well, you're up and walking," said the man, motioning to the woman. "One week ago you hadn't left your bed since we met."

"Yeah..." The woman suddenly realized she was very fatigued. "Can we take a break?" she asked, making her way to a nearby chair.

"You don't have to ask." The man took a seat next to her, leaving one seat in between them.

They sat there in silence for a while until the man asked, "Can I tell you a story?"

"About what?"

"About me, before you met me."

The woman nodded her head. "Sure."

"I used to work as one of the choosers, I may have actually chosen you to be on a Worldship. But I hated my job. I found no purpose in it. And then right as I was about to leave for my Worldship, I was captured and put on trial for my crimes as the people at the time called it. But then I was able to escape those people and get here. But while I was in prison, my mind was going crazy. When I had to walk for two days just to get, here my mind was in even more of a panic. I had some stuff I realized needed worked on, and thanks to these people I got better, but it was a long time before I was fully healed. It was just shortly before you arrived that I got better. And that was only because I had to surrender these thoughts to God, to the people around me who wanted to help. And now I get to share my story with you, as encouragement to show you that you won't always be the way you are right now with God by your side. It takes time, but healing does come."

The woman immediately had an answer ready. "How do you surrender invisible thoughts to an invisible God?"

The man laughed. "It takes faith, a lot of faith. That's also something that doesn't happen over night. It takes time."

"That doesn't make any sense. How is that supposed to help me?"

"It's probably not going to make sense now, but one day you'll understand."

"I want to understand now though, I don't want all of this," the woman motioned to her head, "still running rampant."

The man took a moment before asking, "Can I pray for you?"

"Aren't you already doing that?"

"Yes, but I'd like you to hear the words I speak. They can be an encouragement to you."

"I tried praying before," said the woman, standing up, "it didn't work." The woman paused adding, "Come on, let's finish this tour."

The man stood up with a sigh of grief that the woman thought her prayers hadn't been answered. "You know," said the man, having a revelation, "your prayer may not have been answered, but you should count it a miracle that you're alive."

The woman stopped and turned around. "Why do you say that?"

"You had a forced abortion and then were shot in an escape pod out of the ship and landed right here." The man spread his arms out. "You could have landed anywhere, places far worse than this. There're places I know you would have been used purely to procreate. Some of the population can't do that unfortunately. But look where you are. You have people that love you, care for you, helped you. You have clean clothes and clean water. A roof over your head. God's blessed you with everything you need and more."

The woman took a long time just to sit and process the information only to say, "I need some time to process this."

"I would expect no less," said the man with a smile. "Let's go finish that tour." The man took off and lead the way out of the chapel. "Are you coming," he asked as he turned around in the doorway, finding the woman still frozen in thought.

But the pieces started to click for the woman, specifically about her current situation, and a small grin spread across her face. That grin warmed the man's heart, and he knew the woman was on her way to finding healing.

***

The next three months were filled with lots of questions, revelations, tears, and healing for the woman. The man introduced her to several of his mentors that had helped him through his healing journey. They took time to pray, teach, and inform the woman in all their knowledge. The most impactful to the woman was learning about the current state of the world, and how it truly was a miracle her escape pod landed where it did. Fifty miles in any direction would have put her in a settlement that would have used her for her body, or have been an unlivable death trap.

What was even more impactful, but made the woman really think, was that a calculation had been done based off where her Worldship had launched her escape pod. Accounting for the many errors, it was still concluded that with the trajectory of the escape pod, it was impossible for the woman to have landed where she did.

The questions that led from this discovery were also added to the many questions she had about the several people that counseled her who had had abortions. None of them were forced like her, but willingly. The suffering these women had overcome was a huge encouragement to the woman.

And all these questions, long nights of discussion, tears, anger, and the constant support and love led to the woman starting to regain her life back. She got up one day, without the man bringing her her favorite breakfast, and headed to the outside garden. She walked through the rows of plants and flowers, gently running her hand through their leaves and petals, when the man met her in the garden.

"You know how happy I am to see you up on your own?"

"I'm sure you've been waiting a long time for that day," said the woman with a smile as she turned her head to the man. Ever since the day she crash-landed here, the man had been a constant presence in her life. Encouraging her, answering her questions, crying with her, getting her help from others more knowledgeable than he was. The woman had grown to know the man more than anyone else since her time in the secret place, as everyone else called it.

"Can I ask you a question?" The woman looked the man directly in the eyes.

"Of course."

"Why do you trust in God? Because I put my trust in Him on the Worldship, trusted people I didn't even know. I started believing what they did, acting like they did. Trusting like they did," a tear ran down the woman's cheek, "all for my child not to be here...but I can see now the blessings given to me by the Lord, from how I got here to this healing I am experiencing. You say the Bible talks of God being the same yesterday, today, and tomorrow. So how can I trust the God who was good to me now, and... didn't answer my prayer back then?"

The man found the sitting area in the garden and motioned the woman to sit in the chair next to him as he pondered for a long time how to answer the question. "We don't always know why bad things happen, or why God allows bad things to happen to those who believe in Him. What I do know is that when Eve ate the apple, bringing sin into the world, it hasn't ever been the same. What I believe is that God did not kill your child, just as I know you believe now. Sin killed your child, acted out by man. But God, time and again, has used our greatest pain for his greatest good. You are an encouragement to so many people here. Some were concerned about us taking you in, but now that's not the case. Everyone looks to you as a role model and an example of God's love."

"A role model..." said the woman.

"Yes," said the man with a smile.

The woman smiled with a chuckle, overwhelmed by joy. "Thank you. Thank you for always being there with me. For never giving up on me," the woman looked down, "even after all those times I yelled at you."

"Those things happen, but I've forgiven you. And I'll keep saying that until you believe it in your soul."

The woman smiled again, and for the first time in what felt like forever, the woman cried tears of joy. "I don't think I'd be as healed as I am today without you... can I give you a hug?"

"Of course."

As the two embraced, a wave of peace overwhelmed the woman. And the man began to cry out of reverence and thanks to God. That the soul in front of her was no longer the broken vessel when they had first met.

***

Over the next three months, the woman grew to trust the Lord, a decision she never thought she would ever make. She accepted Christ as her Savior in a chapel service at the altar, and everyone in attendance prayed for hours over her. The next day as a public declaration of faith, the woman was baptized in the lake outside in the valley, being baptized by the man who had pulled her from the escape pod all those days ago.

And seven months after meeting that man, they began dating. At first it was rough as the two initially felt unworthy of the relationship because of their pasts. Especially the man who felt he wasn't worthy of the woman's love; especially after his guilt for being a chooser for the Worldships. But the two, along with support from their friends and mentors, were able to see themselves as Christ does and push past the lies that held then from fully loving each other.

And three months after dating, the two were married. It

was a beautiful day of celebration, love, sacrifice, and reverence to God.

And nine months later, the woman conceived twins, a boy and a girl.

Every day since, the woman has never questioned the love that God has for her. She still misses her nameless child, but she doesn't believe God took her child from her.

Everything that was lost to the woman was restored and more.

Every night the woman and her husband walk outside to watch the sunset, each of them holding one of their children in their arms. Reminded of the beauty, healing, blessings, and restoration that God poured out on their family, and the love of God that is the same yesterday, today, and tomorrow.

A note from the Author

If you've read this book then you've read about a society that controls the birth rate and who can have kids. The main tool they used was abortion and fear. I am not here to tell you whether abortion is right or wrong, I'm here to tell you what the word of God says. I believe every word in the Bible. If you want to know a part of why I believe in the Bible you should read my book *Bondage to Freedom: My 4 year battle with porn and how Jesus was the only cure*. In short, I would not be alive today if it were not for the power and love of Jesus Christ who saved me from death. So when I say I believe in the Bible, I believe it is the living Word of God.

The Bible says that God made us in our mother's womb (Psalm 139:13). We are deeply loved and made by God, from the time of conception when we are a clump of cells until we are born into this world. If God is making us in our mother's womb, isn't abortion stopping God from finishing his creation?

If you want more info on abortion, have had an unplanned pregnancy, or are considering an abortion, I highly encourage you to read through the following resource before you make any decisions. Know the facts.

Option line

Website: Optionline.org
24hr hotline, call or text – 1-800-712-4357

Acknowledgements

I find it hard to write the acknowledgment after what some may consider a heavy book. So I will Thank God and the one other person who helped me put this book in your hands today. Thank you, Kim, my editor, for editing this book. I am truly thankful that we connected and that you get the opportunity to help me bring the words I write to readers wherever they may be. And thank you God for these words, may they be a blessing to all who read them. May they see you and not me.

After dropping out of college to publish my first book, Prime Youth: Prisoners of the Masquerade, at nineteen years old, I haven't looked back. Thank you to all who join me as you read the random words in my head arranged on a page that I hope make sense to someone. Whether you've picked up my sci-fi, memoir, or Young Adult books, I hope you gain something from them. And at the very least, I hope you enjoy.

E.E. Cooley Motto: Creating High Quality, Age-appropriate Experiences

Website: eecooley.com

Instagram: @e.e.cooley

Facebook: E.E. Cooley

Twitter: @EE_Cooley

www.ingramcontent.com/pod-product-compliance
Lightning Source LLC
LaVergne TN
LVHW041533070526
838199LV00046B/1639